Praise for Anne

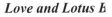

Love and Lotus B...

"Shade imbues this optimistic story of ____ ___-discovery with a refreshing amount of emotional complexity, delivering a queer romance that leans into affection as much as drama, and values friendship and familial love as deeply as romantic connection... Shade's well-drawn Black cast and sophistication in presenting a variety of relationship styles—including open relationships and connections that shift between romance and friendship—creates a rich, affirming, and love-filled setting. (Starred review)" —*Publishers Weekly*

Masquerade

"The atmosphere is brilliant. The way Anne Shade describes the places, the clothes, the vocabulary and turns of phrases she uses carried me easily to Harlem in the 1920s...*Masquerade* is an unexpectedly wild ride, in turns thrilling and chilling. There's nothing more exciting than a woman's quest for freedom and self-discovery."—*Jude in the Stars*

"Heartbreakingly beautiful. This story made me happy and at the same time broke my heart! It was filled with passion and drama that made for an exciting story, packed with emotions that take the reader on quite the ride. It was everything I had expected and so much more. The story was dramatic, and I just couldn't put it down. I had no idea how the story was going to go, and at times I was worried it would all end in a dramatic gangster ending, but that just added to the thrill."—*LezBiReviewed*

"Shade has some moments of genius in this novel where her use of language, descriptions and characters were magnificent."—*Lesbian Review*

Femme Tales

"Shade twines together three sensual novellas, each based on a classic fairy tale and centering black lesbian love...The fairy tale connections put a fun, creative spin on these quick outings. Readers looking for sweet and spicy lesbian romance will be pleased."—*Publishers Weekly*

"If you're a sucker for fairy tales, this trio of racy lesbian retellings is for you. Bringing a modern sensibility to classics like 'Beauty and the Beast,' 'Sleeping Beauty,' and 'Cinderella,' Shade puts a sapphic spin on them that manages to feel realistic."—*Rachel Kramer Bussel, BuzzFeed: 20 Super Sexy Novels Full of Taboo, Kink, Toys, and More*

"All three novellas are quick and easy reads with lovely characters, beautiful settings, and some very steamy romances. They are the perfect stories if you want to sit and escape from the real world for a while and enjoy a bit of fairy tale magic with your romance. I thoroughly enjoyed all three stories."—*Rainbow Reflections*

"I sped through this queer book because the stories were so juicy and sweet, with contemporary storylines that place these characters in Chicago. Each story is packed with tension and smouldering desire with adorably sweet endings. If you're looking for some lesbian romance with B/F dynamic, then these stories are a cute contemporary take on the bedtime stories you loved as a kid, featuring stories exclusively about women of colour."—*Minka Guides*

"Who doesn't love the swagger of a butch or the strength and sass of a femme? All of these characters have depth and are not cardboard cutouts at all. The sense of family is strong through each story and it is probably one of the things I enjoyed most. *Femme Tales* is for every little girl who has grown up wishing for a happy ever after with the Princess, not the Prince."—*Lesbian Review*

By the Author

Femme Tales

Masquerade

Love and Lotus Blossoms

Her Heart's Desire

In Our Words:
Queer Stories from Black, Indigenous and People of Color

Stories Selected by Anne Shade
Edited by Victoria Villaseñor

Visit us at www.boldstrokesbooks.com

HER HEART'S DESIRE

by

Anne Shade

2022

HER HEART'S DESIRE

ISBN 13: 978-1-63679-102-9

This Trade Paperback Original Is Published By
Bold Strokes Books, Inc.
P.O. Box 249
Valley Falls, NY 12185

First Edition: February 2022

Credits
Editor: Cindy Cresap
Production Design: Stacia Seaman
Cover Design by Tammy Seidick

HER HEART'S DESIRE

CHAPTER ONE

Eve struggled with a bag of groceries while attempting to unlock her apartment door. She swore under her breath when her phone began vibrating in her pocket. She threw her keys on the credenza in the foyer, yanked her phone out of her pocket, and tapped the speaker button as she headed to the kitchen.

"Hello."

"Why do you sound so breathless? Please tell me I interrupted you gettin' your groove back," her best friend, Paige, teased her.

Eve looked down at the grocery bags she carried in her other hand. "Unless their name is Häagen-Dazs, nobody's getting any loving here."

Eve could practically feel Paige's breath from the loud, exasperated sigh that followed.

"Are you at least using that vibrator I got you for Christmas?"

Eve shook her head. "Do you think of anything else besides sex?"

"Not really. Why do you think your brother married me? Where else was he gonna find a woman as freaky as I am? Ten years of marriage and we're stilling hittin' it like teenagers."

Eve winced. "I love you both but please spare me the details of your sex life."

"Well, we can't talk about yours since you don't have one. Your stuff is gonna dry up at this rate."

"Paige," Eve groaned.

"Okay, okay. You know I'm just worried about you. You've kept yourself locked up since your divorce. Don't you think you should start putting yourself back out on the market?"

"We've had this conversation before. I have too much going on with Details to worry about my love life."

Details by Eve was her event planning business that she had started two years ago. Thanks to Paige's assistance, the business had taken off and grown quickly in a short time as Crenshaw Associates, Paige's talent agency, hired Eve for all their events and referred Eve to all their business associates.

"I'm not saying you have to get married. I just think you need to go out and start having some fun. Like you did before Stefan came along."

Eve sighed. "If this is what you called for, then you're wasting your breath."

The last thing Eve wanted to talk about was her failed marriage to Stefan Kennedy.

"All right, subject closed…for now. I actually called to throw some business your way."

"Hold on, let me get to my computer." Eve put the last of her groceries away, then walked to her desk.

"I'm ready."

"We need your talents to put together a book release party for a new client."

"Yeah."

"We're looking for something a little different."

"Every event I do is different since each client is different, you know that."

"Well, this client's genre of work isn't something we've not represented before. Her name is Lynette Folsom. She writes lesbian erotica."

Eve's fingers halted over the keyboard. "Oh."

"She's releasing her first book, *Venus's Garden*, at the beginning of Pride week next month."

"When can I meet with her to go over what she's looking to do?"

"Unfortunately, you won't get a chance to meet her until the night of the event. She's out of the country for several weeks for her day job as a tech consultant, so it'll just be you and me, kiddo. I've had a copy of her book sent to you via messenger to help you get your creative juices flowing. I've gotta run to a meeting, but I'll call you later to schedule some time to go over ideas."

"All right, talk to you later."

Eve slumped back into her chair staring at the computer screen but seeing nothing. Their friendship consisted of twenty years of sharing everything from their clothes to their heartaches. When Eve's brother and Paige started dating and eventually married, she was thrilled. Paige had already made herself a part of Eve's family when they met during their sophomore year in high school. But there was one thing Eve had never shared with anyone, including Paige, and now she feared her friend might have unknowingly put her on a path with this event that she wasn't sure she was ready to follow yet.

❖

"Girl, as usual, you've managed to pull off another masterpiece," Paige said, gazing around the room.

"I just hope your client likes it. I really wish we could've met to get her input on our plans."

"You mean your plans. I just nodded and let you do your thing. I guess sending you Lynette's book really did get those juices flowing."

"You have no idea," Eve said under her breath.

"What?"

"Oh, I was just saying yeah, what a great idea."

Paige gazed at her curiously. "Well, I think she'll love it. You did a great job. I'm gonna give her a call to find out what's keeping her."

"I'll go check on the caterers." Eve headed toward the back of the art gallery they had rented for the event.

She had to admit that this was one of the most unique events she'd planned. The theme was "A Night of Sensuality" to go along with the genre of the book. They chose the gallery because of the erotic art exhibit on display. The entertainment was a live jazz band known for the sultry voice of their lead singer; the menu consisted of lobster, oysters, shrimp, strawberries, chocolate, and many other items known for their aphrodisiac qualities. The servers, dressed in long toga-style dresses tied over one shoulder with a thigh-high slit up the leg, were all tall, voluptuous women from a local modeling agency. They rented low cushioned chairs, tables, and ottomans that were dispersed throughout the room and set up special lighting that bathed it in a soft glow with subtle intermittent color changes throughout the night. The environment oozed eroticism, which Paige claimed was her client's only request. After reading *Venus's Garden*, Eve could see why.

❖

As Lynette Folsom walked into the gallery, she was greeted by her slightly annoyed agent.

"It's about time," Paige reprimanded her.

Lynette grinned. "You didn't think I was going to miss my own party?"

"Last time we spoke you said you'd just gotten off a flight from London and would call me after you got some sleep. That was a day ago."

"Yeah, I apologize for that. I turned all lines of communication off so I wouldn't get any interruptions. I didn't want to end up suffering from jet lag and crash in a corner of the room."

"Well, we've got about fifteen minutes before we officially open the doors, so why don't we do a quick run-through of the evening."

Lynette followed Paige around the gallery as she described what the event entailed. She was very impressed and couldn't have done better if she'd planned it herself. The setup was sexy without being vulgar. Paige had told her to leave the planning in her hands, and Lynette was glad she had.

"This is great, Paige. It's far more than I expected."

"I can't take all of the credit. My girl Eve did ninety-nine-point-nine percent of it. I did book the band, though," Paige said proudly.

Lynette chuckled. "Please be sure to thank her for me."

"You can do that yourself. Let me introduce you."

They walked toward one of three bars that had been set up and a woman whose back was toward them as she spoke with the bartender. Lynette saw a full, curvaceous figure nicely enveloped in a sleeveless black silk wrap dress that came to just above her knees. When she stood on tiptoe to look at something on the other side of the bar, Lynette's gaze traveled the length of her torso, down her rounded behind, to her smooth legs and the strappy, high-heeled sandals on her feet. If this woman looked as good from the front as she did from the back, Lynette was in trouble.

"Eve, our guest of honor finally arrived," Paige announced.

"Great. I can't wait to find out what she thinks." Eve turned around and Lynette's heart skipped a beat at the sight of her beautiful smile.

"Eve Monroe, I'd like you to meet Lynette Folsom," Paige said.

Lynette smiled, thinking that if the original Eve looked anything like this woman, she could see why Adam fell from grace. Eve's shoulder-length hair lay in soft, golden brown curls framing her heart-shaped face. Her complexion was the color of rich caramel, and she had almond-shaped, light brown eyes. Her only makeup seemed to be a wine-colored lipstick that made her full lips appear to be more luscious.

She offered Eve her hand. "Thank you for all of this."

Eve accepted it and Lynette felt a spark at the contact. "You're welcome. Reading your book gave me the idea."

"You read it? What did you think?"

"I enjoyed it very much. Your writing is very…vivid," Eve said, smiling shyly.

Lynette chuckled. "Vivid, huh. I like that."

"Well, we better get your signing table set up," Paige interrupted them. "People will be arriving any minute."

Eve slowly slid her soft, warm hand from Lynette's grasp. Lynette hadn't even realized she was still holding it. "Enjoy the party. I'll be here the entire time, so don't hesitate to let me know if you need anything."

"I'll do that. See you later," Lynette said, hesitantly turning to follow Paige.

❖

Eve watched Lynette walk away admiring her casual but stylish dress; slow, easy stride; and athletic build. Lynette wore a pair of black jeans that hugged her slim hips, rounded behind, and long legs, a caramel color button-down suede shirt that looked great against her smooth dark complexion. Matching suede loafers finished the look. The sight of the tight waves in her close-cropped hair made Eve's fingertips itch to run over them.

"Get a hold of yourself, girl," she said under her breath, but found she couldn't tear her eyes from Lynette's retreating figure.

When Lynette and Paige stopped at the table set aside for her to sign books, she glanced back at Eve, grinning knowingly. Eve forced herself to slowly turn away and walk, instead of run, to the ladies' room. Her attraction to Lynette was instantaneous the moment she turned around, and Eve had lost all train of thought as she gazed into the deepest brown eyes she'd ever seen. Putting a face to the woman who had put such erotic images in Eve's mind was a little more overwhelming than she had expected. Was she hoping that Lynette would be the nerdy, bookish-looking woman she'd imagined when Paige told her Lynette was in the technology industry? Maybe. At least then she wouldn't be standing in the bathroom holding a cool, wet towel to her cheeks to stave off the rush of desire she felt at the thought of wondering if Lynette wrote the steamy sex scenes in her book from experience or a vivid imagination.

Eve gazed at her reflection in the mirror. "Okay, you need to get yourself together, shrug off your horny divorcee cloak, put your planner hat on, and do your best to avoid the very attractive and sexy Lynette Folsom the whole night."

Satisfied with her personal pep talk, Eve nodded, took a deep breath, and left the ladies' room feeling more like herself.

❖

Lynette sat in her office staring down at Eve's business card wondering whether to call her. She'd picked up vibes that Eve was attracted to her, but Paige made it quite clear when she'd asked if Eve was in a relationship that she didn't date women. Either Paige didn't know her friend as well as she thought, or Lynette had misread the signals she was getting from Eve. They barely had a chance to say two words to each other once the party started, but she'd caught Eve glancing in her direction too many times to be coincidence. After the event was over, Lynette made it a point to ask Eve for her card before she left. That was almost a week ago and she couldn't get Eve off her mind. Lynette picked up her phone, called Eve's number, and was a bit relieved to get her voice mail.

"Hey, Eve. It's Lynette Folsom. I just wanted to thank you again for a great party. I hope you'll let me take you to dinner or for drinks in appreciation of all your hard work. Give me a call when you get the chance."

Lynette left her office and cell number, then hung up. She'd done her part. The ball was now in Eve's court.

❖

Eve looked down at her watch. She'd just finished a meeting with a local councilwoman planning a fundraiser that took much longer than expected. Now she was going to be late for her next client meeting. She was supposed to meet with a bride and groom in fifteen minutes about the final arrangements for their wedding that weekend. There was no way she was making it from Brooklyn to Harlem in time. She was going to have to reschedule for later that afternoon.

Reaching into her bag for her phone, she noticed one missed call. She didn't recognize the number so decided to check the voice mail after she called her client. Unfortunately, the bride wasn't very understanding and told her she'd give her an hour to get there rather than reschedule, so her voice mail would have to wait until she got home.

Three hours, and one happy bride later, Eve arrived home, kicked off her shoes, turned on her Bluetooth speaker, flopped back on the sofa, and let the soothing sound of jazz music wash over her before she dialed her voice mail. As she listened to the message, Eve's eyes widened in surprise. Although she'd been thinking about her since the night of the party, Lynette Folsom was the last person Eve expected to hear from.

Paige mentioned Lynette's interest and how she'd told her Eve didn't date women, so she assumed that was the end of it. Obviously, she was wrong because Lynette was asking her out. Eve shook her head. She was reading too much into it. After all, Lynette didn't mention anything about a date. She said she wanted to thank her for the party. If Paige told her Eve wasn't interested in women, then she wouldn't waste her time by asking her out on a date. Would she? Was it possible that she picked up on Eve's attraction that night despite what Paige told her? She should just call Lynette, thank her politely and tell her she wasn't interested. But Eve found she didn't want to.

She called Lynette.

"Hello."

"Hi, Lynette. It's Eve Monroe." She hoped her voice didn't sound as shaky as she felt.

"Hey, Eve. Hold on for a sec."

Eve heard muffled talking then some shuffling before Lynette got back on the line.

"Sorry about that."

"Did I call you at a bad time?"

"Oh, no. I was paying the delivery guy for my food."

"Oh, okay. Well, I was just returning your call about going to dinner. I'd like that."

"Great. I'm available this weekend. What's your schedule look like?"

"I'm available after five Saturday night. I have an early wedding that day."

"Great, Saturday it is. Will seven work for you?"

"That's fine. Gives me time to rest and recover. Weddings are a killer. Fortunately, I love what I do."

"You're very good at what you do. Being able to understand what people want and making it come to life for them is pretty cool."

Eve felt her face heat with a blush. "Thanks. It's not as special as being able to make your words come to life. I got so caught up in your stories that I could practically feel each embrace and touch."

"That's one of the best reviews I've received so far. Thank you."

"You're welcome. Well, I'll let you get to your dinner."

"Speaking of dinner, where should we meet?"

After deciding on a place to meet and saying their good-byes, Eve attempted to dispel the nervous fluttering in her stomach as she tried to convince herself that it was simply a "thank you" dinner from a satisfied client, nothing more. Eve could no longer deny the truth. She was, and had always been, hopelessly attracted to women. She'd fought the feelings for so long that, for a little while, she'd managed to convince herself that it was just a minor curiosity at best.

She should've known better when she tried appeasing that curiosity back in high school and college and all it did was make her want more. Instead of accepting it for what it was and allowing herself to explore her feelings further, she went in the opposite direction because of fear of how her family would react if she admitted to her attraction to women as well as men. Especially after the way her mother's family in Puerto Rico reacted when her cousin Julian admitted to being gay.

Eve's mother had grown up in a very strict Catholic family, and although her mother loosened up her moral compass after moving to the United States, her family, especially her sister, Cecelia, Julian's mother, were still just as devout as ever. Even after Julian came out, his mother had ignored the truth for as long as she could until Julian became more open and honest about who he was. Now it had been almost twenty years since they'd seen or spoken to each other. Eve didn't believe her parents would go to such extremes, but she also knew her mother well enough to know that she might not be accepting of it, her brothers probably wouldn't be thrilled, and her family in Puerto Rico would be just as unaccepting as they had been of Julian. Eve was close with her brothers and both parents, but the bond she had with her mother was one she wasn't willing to risk losing.

Eve met Stefan, her ex-husband or Mr. Perfect as Paige called him, in college and coldly cut ties with a woman she'd been having a discreet liaison with at the time without any explanation. She hadn't felt she needed one since, in her confused mind, they weren't a real couple. Eve had thrown herself into her relationship with Stefan, doing all she could to ignore her true feelings. She married him, doing what she believed was the socially acceptable way to live the life her parents wanted for her and attempted to become the perfect doctor's wife by putting all her dreams of becoming a corporate event planner aside to help Stefan start his private practice. She maintained her charade for the first five years of their marriage until a new patient walked into the office. It was the woman

Eve had been involved with in college. She hadn't recognized her name when she made the appointment because, like Eve, she'd gotten married.

Seeing her previous lover again, looking just as good as she did in college, brought back all those feelings Eve had managed to keep locked away for the past ten years. At the woman's insistence, they met for drinks. She told Eve she didn't blame her for the way things ended. She had been just as confused about their affair as Eve had. As the night wore on and the drinks flowed, Eve found herself flirting with the woman. It wasn't long before they wound up at a hotel getting reacquainted with the passion that brought them together so many years before.

Their affair went on for six months before it came to a screeching halt after Stefan, who knew of Eve's brief affair with a woman in college but not who the woman had been, became suspicious of Eve spending so much time with a mysterious new friend and decided to go through her phone while she was in the shower one morning. Eve had never gotten around to setting up her phone lock, so he had easy access to all her text messages to and from her lover. When he confronted her, Eve could see that Stefan wanted her to deny it, explain that it was a mistake. He probably would've believed anything she told him just so that he didn't have to face the truth, but she didn't. She told him everything but who the woman was since he was still her doctor.

Stefan was devastated, but even he had to admit that the past several years of their marriage had them living more like roommates than a married couple, so their divorce was lengthy but amicable. They sold their house in Jersey. She received half from the sale, as well as a quarter of what the medical practice was worth. Despite Eve's feelings that she'd deserved so much more with all she'd given up for, and put into, the practice, she took it without complaint.

After what she had done, Stefan could've dragged her through the mud, but he hadn't, so she just wanted to be free of it all. She'd spent so many years trying to be what Stefan wanted and what her mother had hoped for that she'd lost sight of her true self. Since then, she'd thrown herself into her business to avoid thinking about her nonexistent love life. Now her love life was insinuating itself back into the spotlight in a way she would've never expected.

CHAPTER TWO

Filled with nervous energy about their dinner, Lynette stood in front of the restaurant waiting for Eve to arrive. As much as she hoped Eve was interested in her, she wondered if she really wanted to start dating a woman who was obviously not out. She'd been down that road before and it had not ended well.

Lynette had planned to keep the dinner conversation casual until she spotted Eve walking toward her. She had a natural sexiness about her that drew Lynette like a bee to pollen. She wore a sleeveless burgundy silk sheath dress that hit her calves and molded to her curvaceous figure and a pair of platform heeled sandals with ribbon ties wrapped around her ankles. As she drew closer, Lynette could see she wore little makeup accept that wine-colored lipstick she'd worn when they first met. It had Lynette licking her own lips in anticipation.

"Down, girl," she mumbled to herself.

"Hi, I'm not late, am I?" Eve asked, gazing down at her watch.

Lynette held the door open for her. "No, you're right on time. I just got here a few minutes ago."

Eve walked in ahead of her, and Lynette watched the sway of her hips beneath the smooth material of the dress, in appreciation. It was still early for a Saturday night, so the restaurant wasn't crowded, and they were seated right away. To Lynette's chagrin, of all the places they could have been seated, they were taken to an intimate candlelit table in the corner.

"Is this okay?" she asked Eve, hoping she didn't read anything into the romantic seating.

Eve smiled. "It's fine."

Something in the way Eve was looking at her had Lynette's curiosity piqued. Had she read Eve's signals correctly the night of the party? When the waiter took their drink order Lynette thought it would be best to play it safe by not drinking any alcohol. She needed all her senses sharp this evening.

"Thank you again for the terrific job you did on the party," Lynette said.

"You're welcome. I'm glad you enjoyed it. I was worried it might've been a bit over the top."

"Not at all, I just wish I hadn't been traveling for work. We could've met sooner. It would've been nice working together and being a part of the planning."

"Well, you were a part of it in some way. All my ideas were a result of reading *Venus's Garden*."

"Was there any particular story that stood out for you more than the others?"

Eve looked thoughtful for a moment. "They were all great. I guess my favorite would be 'Quiet Storm.' I can identify with what the character Lily was going through."

"Really?" Lynette said in surprise.

She felt the urge to jump up and start pumping her fist in excitement. *Quiet Storm* was about a woman who tried to be the good little Catholic girl, but her attraction to women kept her from having any serious relationships with men. Tired of fighting her feelings, she went to a gay bar with the intention of picking up a woman and appeasing whatever the feelings were so that she could move on with her life. But to her surprise, she met a woman named Alex whose gentle passion showed her that her attraction couldn't be so easily dismissed. For Eve to admit she identified with Lily proved, in Lynette's mind, that she hadn't been wrong about her.

"Can I ask you a very personal question?"

"Go ahead." Eve fidgeted with her napkin but didn't take her gaze from Lynette's.

"Paige said you weren't interested in dating women. Was she right?"

Eve began to answer but was interrupted by the waiter with their drinks. He prolonged the moment by taking their order. Lynette couldn't wait for him to leave. Once he did, she turned her attention back to Eve.

"No, she wasn't."

"I take it she doesn't know about your attraction to women."

"No. Honestly, I'm still trying to accept it myself," Eve admitted with a sigh.

"Is this just a curiosity thing?" Lynette didn't want to be somebody's sexual experiment.

"No. Like Lily, it's always been there, I've just been trying to be the good little Catholic girl and fight it. My mother was raised by a strict Catholic mother who almost disowned her when she chose to stay here and marry my Baptist African American father instead of going back to Puerto Rico and marrying a good Catholic boy of her own race. Although she's not the devout Catholic my grandmother was, I'm fairly sure she would not be accepting of her daughter dating women."

"Oh." Lynette sure knew how to pick them, a closeted lesbian from a homophobic Catholic family.

They sat silently for a moment, lost in their own thoughts.

"I have to ask," Eve said, breaking the silence. "Why did you ask me to dinner?"

"Honestly? Because I was attracted to you and thought I'd picked up on a similar feeling from you the night of the party. Was I mistaken?"

Eve gave her a shy smile. "No, you weren't. But what if you had been?"

Lynette shrugged. "I would have apologized and hoped that we could be friends."

"And now that you know you were right?"

Lynette grinned. "I hope that we can get to know each other and take it from there. No pressure."

Eve's smile broadened. "I'd like that."

Eve's honesty seemed to help both to relax and enjoy the evening. They talked about their childhoods and found that they shared similar backgrounds growing up with religion as a heavy influence in their lives. With Lynette it was through her Baptist upbringing and for Eve, her Catholic. Although both of their parents were still together, Eve, the only girl, was the middle of five children, while Lynette, the oldest of her siblings, had a brother and sister. They even found they shared the same social and political ideals. They were clicking so well that Lynette was beginning to wonder if it was all too good to be true. Eve was sweet, smart, easygoing, opinionated, and sexy as hell. It was reminiscent of how she and her ex, Marisol, had clicked so well when they first met, and that hadn't turned out as well as she had expected.

As they finished dessert, she realized they'd talked about everything but their previous relationships. Lynette figured this had to be Eve's first real date with a woman and wondered if she'd ever been intimate with one. She didn't want to ruin the vibe by asking, so she decided to save the question for another time. If she was honest with herself, she was also just afraid of finding out something she really didn't want to know.

"You realize we've been sitting here for three hours?" Eve said.

Lynette chuckled. "That explains why the waiter seemed annoyed the last time he came to check on us." She looked around, then signaled him for the check.

"I had a great time, Lynette," Eve said as they left the restaurant.

"Enough to want to go out again?" Lynette asked hopefully.

Eve didn't hesitate in answering. "Yes."

"Great. I'll call you during the week to set something up."

"Okay. Enjoy the rest or your weekend," Eve said, turning to walk away.

"Eve."

Eve turned back toward her. "Yes."

Lynette took the few steps that separated them and, hoping that she wouldn't get slapped for what she was about to do, placed a soft kiss on Eve's lips.

"I'll talk to you soon," she said, slowly backing away, leaving a dazed-looking Eve gazing back at her.

❖

Eve couldn't sleep. She looked over at the bedside clock with a frustrated sigh. It was after midnight and she lay in bed thinking about her evening with Lynette. Lynette had surprised her with her blunt questions. Even more, she'd surprised herself with her answers. She could also still feel the heated imprint of Lynette's lips on hers. The evening had turned out much different than she'd expected. Lynette was so easy to be with that Eve didn't feel the awkwardness or pressure that could come from a first date. It felt so natural.

Her phone buzzing on her nightstand jarred Eve out of her thoughts. When she saw Lynette's name she quickly sat up and grabbed her phone to answer it.

"Hello."

"Hi, it's Lynette. Were you sleeping?"

Eve's heart skipped a bit at the sound of Lynette's deep voice. It recalled the smooth notes of a saxophone in the jazz music she loved. "No, just lying here. What's up?"

"I apologize for calling so late. I really enjoyed myself tonight and wanted to talk to you about something before we went out again."

"Sure, what is it?" Eve stacked her pillows behind her back and sat up against the headboard.

"I really like you. I think we've got a connection that I'd be crazy to ignore."

Eve grinned happily. "I feel the same way."

"That's good to hear. With that said, I need to tell you about my last relationship. Up until two years ago, I was with a woman who I was planning to marry and start a family with."

There was a pause on the other end that made Eve nervous. She prayed Lynette wasn't about to tell her that she was going back to an ex-girlfriend. Not after she'd decided to explore her feelings for her.

Lynette continued. "Just as we began making plans for our future together, she told me that she'd been having second thoughts about our relationship and had been trying to find a way to tell me that she'd been seeing a man for the last year of the five years we'd been together."

"Wow." Eve didn't know what else to say, especially knowing what she'd done that ended her marriage.

"I shouldn't have been surprised because she was going through a bad divorce when we started seeing each other. We worked together and were friends at the office. One day I could see she really needed to talk, so I suggested we go for drinks after work. She offered to cook dinner instead and I accepted. We were talking, she started crying, I held her, she kissed me, and one thing led to another. I'd always been attracted to her but left it alone since she was married. Not long after her divorce she moved in with me and I thought, other than her family not agreeing with her lifestyle, that we were doing great. Then, in the midst of planning our future together, she tells me that she loved me but couldn't bear the thought of raising children in a relationship like ours."

Eve could hear the pain in Lynette's voice. "You don't have to talk about this now if it's too difficult."

"I need to tell you this so you'll understand when I say that I can't do that again. After that happened, I promised myself that I wouldn't get involved with straight or closeted females. I need to know, even if we're just casually dating, that she's not going to turn around and decide she's ashamed of our relationship or that she wants to be with a man. I want to be with a woman who wants to truly be with me and not simply experimenting or appeasing her curiosity," Lynette said.

Eve was silent for a moment, unsure of whether Lynette would fit her into any of those categories. She knew that despite having been with men in the past, and having been married, the idea of doing so again no longer appealed to her and she honestly believed it never would again. But she was still in the closet. Well, after tonight, she'd at least put her foot out the door, but she didn't know if it would be enough for Lynette.

"Are you still there?" Lynette asked.

"Yes, just thinking about what you said."

"I know that was a lot to throw at you after just one dinner, and I wouldn't be surprised if it was our last, but I needed to put that out there. I hope you understand."

Eve could hear the guarded tone in Lynette's voice and knew she must've thought her lack of response meant Eve was no longer interested.

"I understand completely, and I appreciate your honesty. Since you've been so honest with me it's only fair that I do the same."

Eve told Lynette about Stefan, her brief affair, and why her marriage ultimately ended not because of the affair but because Eve was tired of lying to herself.

"I'm very much attracted to you," she told Lynette, "and I would like for us to get to know each other, but I need to take it one step at a time. So, I hope you don't write me off as one of those closeted women you don't want to be involved with, but if you feel my not being out is something you can't deal with, I understand."

Eve heard nothing but silence on the other end of the phone until Lynette said, "So when are you free again?"

Eve did a seated happy dance. "My next three Fridays and Saturdays are booked for weddings, but Sunday through Thursday look good."

They made plans to spend the day in the Hamptons the following Sunday.

"I'll let you get back to bed. Good night, Eve."

"Good night, Lynette."

Eve hung up, sighing contentedly as she curled back up under the covers, hugging the body pillow she kept in bed with her. Lynette was charming, understanding, and had a seductive quality about her that drew Eve. There were several times throughout their dinner that she had to keep from staring at Lynette's long, neatly manicured fingers as she wondered what they would feel like on her body. Eve's nipples hardened in response to the intimate thoughts. She hugged the body pillow tighter, wishing it were Lynette. Her body grew warm, and a shaky sigh escaped as she licked her suddenly dry lips. Wrapping her legs around the pillow, she moaned aloud as it brushed up against the crotch of her underwear. She moved her hips slowly, causing a soft friction against her clit. Eve bit her bottom lip as a shiver of pleasure gently racked her body.

She rarely pleasured herself. When she did it was out of pure desperation. This time was different. The need was purely for pleasure's sake. She set the body pillow aside, rolled onto her back, and pulled her nightshirt and underwear off. Moving her hands softly across her body, she imagined they were Lynette's hands, gripping her breast and teasing her hardened nipples. Lynette's long, manicured, fingers sliding down past her abdomen, to the triangle between her legs, spreading her lips and dipping into the moist heat within. It was Lynette's face Eve saw in her mind's eye as her body shook, and she cried out with her release.

❖

Lynette lay in bed staring at her phone trying not to think about if she was making a mistake in getting involved with Eve. While she appreciated Eve being so straightforward about where she was in her acceptance of her sexuality, Lynette was hesitant to put herself out there again with a woman who might not have fully accepted herself or had the acceptance of her family. She knew that not every lesbian she would date would have a family as accepting as most of hers was, but she also knew that a family's unacceptance of a person's sexuality could seriously affect how they saw themselves, which affected how secure they were in their romantic relationships.

Lynette didn't really know Eve yet, but it was difficult

not to compare her to her ex, Marisol, whose family saw her relationship with Lynette as a rebound from, and a result of, her unhappy marriage and divorce. They were cordial to Lynette, but she could see in their eyes what she had failed to see herself. That it wouldn't last. That their daughter was simply trying something different to ease the hurt her ex-husband had caused.

Marisol had claimed she'd never been with a woman before but had always been curious, which should've been a red flag, but Lynette let her own infatuation with her blind her to that, how Marisol's parents were, and what her own family tried to tell her. Lynette had managed to keep those blinders on their entire relationship and only had herself to blame for being blindsided by Marisol breaking her heart.

Lynette set her phone back on the nightstand, lay down, and thought about her evening with Eve and the conversation they just had. Eve had been honest about her situation, which Lynette appreciated, but it still didn't waylay the worry of getting involved with her. Like Marisol, she'd been married before and wasn't wholly accepting of her sexuality. Unlike Marisol, Eve had been with women in the past, although never openly, and said she had no desire to be involved with a man again.

That should have been enough for Lynette not to stress herself over, especially since this was only going to be their first date, but heartbreak could make you overly cautious. An image of Eve's sexy smile came unbidden to Lynette's mind, making her smile as well. To be gifted with that smile, to feel those soft lips pressed to her own once again, had Lynette deciding to throw caution to the wind and wait to see where it would lead her.

❖

The following evening, Eve sat at her computer going over her upcoming event schedule when the doorman buzzed her to let her know that she had a delivery, and that Paige was there.

Eve unlocked the door for Paige, then grabbed a bottle of wine that she'd been chilling in the refrigerator. Since their college days, she and Paige had a standing date one Sunday a month to get together, eat Chinese food, drink wine, and have their own Black Film Festival.

"Special delivery for Ms. Eve Monroe," Paige announced as she walked into the apartment.

"Come on in the living room, I've got everything set up. All we have to do is lay the food out and press play," Eve said.

To her surprise, Paige walked in with a bouquet of long-stemmed, pink roses.

"You were just supposed to bring the food. I wasn't expecting flowers too," she said, chuckling.

Paige was grinning broadly. "They're not from me. This is the delivery Frank was telling you about."

Eve walked over and took the roses from Paige. "There must be a mistake." She looked for a card.

"I doubt it unless there's another Eve Monroe in the building." Paige playfully waved the small card she must have taken from the bouquet.

"Well, open it while I put them in water. They're probably from the bride and groom whose wedding I did yesterday," she said, walking back to the kitchen.

Paige followed her, setting the bag of Chinese food on the counter and opening the card.

"Eve, thank you for last night and please keep this quote in mind until we see each other again, *If I could have a rose for every time I thought of you, the world would be empty of them*, Truly, Lynette."

As Paige had been reading the card Eve's heart practically stopped. Now a deafening silence filled the room as she gathered the nerve to turn around and meet Paige's questioning gaze.

"Paige, I…" Eve struggled to find the words.

"I think I need that glass of wine now." Paige turned and left the room.

Taking a deep breath, Eve followed her. She waited for Paige to pour and take a rather large sip of wine before she spoke.

"We need to talk."

"Obviously," Paige said with nervous laughter. "First, tell me if Lynette is the same Lynette I think she is?"

"Yes." Eve sat beside Paige.

Paige took another large drink from her glass, emptied it, and then poured another. "Okay, I'm ready."

"After the book release party Lynette called to thank me and asked to take me to dinner to show her appreciation. That's what *last night* referred to on the card," Eve explained. "Later that night she called me, we talked on the phone for a while, and she asked me to go out with her again."

"She's gay, Eve."

"I'm fully aware of that. You're the one that told me, remember?"

Paige frowned. "Are you attracted to her?"

"Yes."

"Is this because of Stefan? I read somewhere that a lot of women tend to get a little freaky after divorce, especially if they weren't satisfied in their marriage."

Eve shook her head. "This has nothing to do with Stefan or my divorce. Well, actually, it does, but not in the way you're thinking."

"Okay, my head is spinning. I shouldn't have had that wine." Paige put the glass on the coffee table and picked up a bottle of water Eve had put out as well. "Just answer one question. Are you gay, bisexual, or what?"

"I guess I'm bisexual."

"If you have to guess then maybe you aren't. Maybe it's just been too long since you've been with someone, and I even have to admit that Lynette is hot," she said with a weak smile.

Eve shook her head. "I've been more attracted to women than men for as long as I can remember," Eve admitted, relieved that she no longer had to keep that secret from her best friend.

"Why now? Did Lynette seduce you? I knew there was something about the way she kept watching you that night. Is that what this is all about?" Paige asked angrily.

"Paige, this is about me. I've kept this inside for so long that I'd even convinced myself that it wasn't true, that it was just a curiosity, but I was wrong. It's been more than that and I've known it since before Stefan and I met. Remember Charise Turner?"

"Yeah, that girl you suddenly started hanging out with every now and then back in college?" Paige's eyes grew wide in disbelief. "You and Charise!"

Eve nodded. "It only went on for a few months, then I met Stefan and stopped seeing her until she came to his office as a new patient. We were having an affair and Stefan found out."

"Aw, Eve." Paige rubbed her hand across her eyes.

"He wanted me to tell him it was just a thing. That it would never happen again, but I couldn't. I was tired of lying to him and myself. Paige, you're the one who's always telling me that I have to be true to myself and not live my life by someone else's standards. Well, that's what I'm finally doing, and I need you to be just as supportive now as you've been all these years."

Paige gave her a look of understanding. "Eve, you're my best friend and my sister-in-law. I can't imagine what my life would've been like without you in it and sure as hell don't want to find out now. So whatever support you need, I'm here."

Eve took Paige's hand. "You don't know how much that means to me. I was so worried you wouldn't take this well."

"Well, I can't say I'm not thrown for a loop, but I figure you're going to need all the backup you can get. When you tell your mother she's gonna be calling the nearest priest to perform an exorcism on you because you're obviously possessed by something," Paige said with a grin.

Eve frowned thoughtfully. "I'm not ready to tell anyone else in the family yet, so this will have to stay between us until I am."

"Girl, you know my lips are sealed, but I do have one last question."

"Yes?"

"Are you sure about this? You know it's not gonna be easy, and I'm not just talking about your family."

"I'm as sure as I can be right now. I'm taking it one day at a time."

"And Lynette? Are you ready for a relationship with her?"

"I don't know. Like I said, one day at a time. I know this is going to sound strange, but in the brief time we've spent together I've felt more feminine and freer to be myself than I have with any man," Eve said with a smile.

"I haven't seen you smile like that in a long time. Just be careful. Whether you're gay or straight, you can still get your heart broken."

❖

Lynette received a call from Paige's assistant shortly after she got into work being summoned to a meeting with Paige that very afternoon, and she had a pretty good idea why.

"Hey, Paige, I got your message about the interview with *OUT* magazine. That's exciting," Lynette said as she walked into Paige's office.

"Yeah, they're doing a special on up-and-coming authors of Color. I just need your travel schedule for work so we can plan around it to set up the interview."

Paige's usually friendly tone was very businesslike, and she didn't look the least bit pleased to see Lynette despite being the one who requested the meeting.

"Do you want to talk about what's really on your mind?" Lynette asked.

"What do you mean? We're talking about your schedule, aren't we?"

"We could've done that over the phone since I was at my office. Eve told me she spoke to you about our seeing each other."

Paige sat back in her chair, arms crossed, her gaze narrowed at Lynette.

"Eve is going through a pretty confusing time right now, which makes her vulnerable to someone who might want to take advantage of her. I won't stand by and watch that happen. So, if that's your intention you might as well walk away now because I won't hesitate to do whatever it takes to protect her from getting hurt. Understood?"

"Please be assured that I have only the best intentions with Eve. She's a special woman who I'm genuinely interested in," Lynette reassured her. "Although, if you're uncomfortable with the situation and feel it might affect how you represent me, then maybe someone else from the firm should."

Paige was thoughtful for a moment before she nodded.

"I'll have Eric take over. He's one of my best agents and is familiar with what we've done so far. Let me get him in here so we can make sure we're on the same page."

Lynette truly regretted losing Paige as her agent. She liked her and the way she handled herself, but she understood. Lynette just hoped losing one of the best talent agents in the business was worth the chance she was taking with Eve.

"He thinks and works along the same lines I do, so you won't miss me at all," Paige said, as if reading Lynette's thoughts. "Besides, you're not completely out of hot water. You're seeing my best friend, so I'll be keeping an eye on you."

Lynette smiled. "I'd do the same thing if I were in your place."

"Now that we know where we stand, let's get back to business," Paige suggested as Lynette's new agent, Eric Saunders, walked in.

CHAPTER THREE

Eve grabbed her beach bag and the cooler with the lunch she'd prepared for her and Lynette's afternoon at the beach before walking out of her apartment. Lynette was waiting in front of the building leaning against a candy apple red Mustang GT convertible.

Grinning, Lynette opened the passenger door for Eve. "Your chariot awaits, my lady."

Eve laughed. "So, this is the toy you told me about?"

"Yep," she said, taking Eve's bag and cooler and placing it in the back seat.

When Eve sank into the plush leather seats, she was enveloped by new car smell.

"You told me you only brought this car out for special occasions," she said as Lynette got in.

"That's true. As a matter of fact, this is only the third time I've driven it since I bought it earlier this year."

"I'm flattered."

Lynette turned to her. "So am I. This is a big step for you, and you chose to take it with me. You deserve to go in style."

"Thank you."

They gazed at one another for a moment before Lynette turned and pulled the car away from the curb.

"I'm sorry about your losing Paige as an agent. I feel like it's my fault."

"I told you before that you have nothing to apologize for. Everything worked out fine. Paige was right about Eric. I couldn't have asked for a better replacement. I'm scheduled for an interview with *OUT*, a book signing at Giovanni's Room in Philly, and a speaking engagement at an upcoming LGBTQ event."

"So, you're okay with it?" It was difficult for Eve not to feel responsible.

"I'm fine. I'm still being represented by one of the best agencies in New York, my book is selling like hotcakes, and I'm spending the day at the beach with a beautiful woman. What more could I ask for?"

Eve felt her face heat with a blush. "Well, when you put it that way, how could I feel bad?"

The hour-long drive to Long Island flew by as Eve and Lynette talked. They had spent every night since their dinner on the phone, sometimes for hours, with their conversations traveling from one subject to the next. Today was no different and she thoroughly enjoyed it.

As they neared their destination, Lynette put the top down on the car and Eve threw her head back to enjoy the warmth of the sun on her face. Lynette was hard-pressed to keep her eyes on the road. Her gaze kept wandering over to Eve, who seemed to blossom under the sun's adoration. The beach was already crowded, so it took them some time to find parking and a spot on the sand. Once they did, Eve laid out a large blanket she'd brought, and two beach chairs Lynette had supplied while she set up the beach umbrella they rented.

Once they were finished, Lynette was given an eyeful as Eve shed her T-shirt and shorts. She wore a subtle leopard print two-piece halter tankini with a V-neckline that made Lynette want to cover her back up so that no one else's mouth would begin watering like hers. Every man and woman within sight of them couldn't help but admire how sexy she was.

Eve seemed oblivious to the effect she was having on Lynette, or anyone else, as she neatly folded her clothes, then knelt to put them in her bag. When she completed her task, she gazed up at Lynette curiously.

"What's wrong?"

Lynette managed to tear her eyes away, trying to make it look as if she were searching for something in her own bag.

"I need my sunscreen. It's really hot." Lynette was glad she was a woman because if she'd been a man there would have been no getting away with that lie. Her physical reaction to Eve would have been obvious.

"Do you want a bottle of water?" Eve asked in concern.

"No, I'm good. The shade under the umbrella is helping already," Lynette reassured her with a smile.

"Drink this anyway." Eve handed her a bottle of water from the cooler. "Did you eat anything this morning?"

"Eve, I'm fine, really. To be honest it wasn't the heat that overcame me," Lynette admitted with a guilty grin. "It's your bathing suit."

Eve was confused for a moment, then a blush crept over her face. "Oh." She reached for her T-shirt. "I knew it was too much, but the saleslady insisted it looked great on me."

Lynette stopped her from putting the shirt on. "She was right." She gave Eve an appreciative glance.

A shy smile crossed Eve's face. "Really? I've gained some weight since my divorce and had to get a new bathing suit."

"You have nothing to worry about. If you could've seen

the look on all these men's faces when you undressed, you would know that I'm not the only one that likes the added curves."

Eve laughed. "Now you're exaggerating."

"You think so? How about I go test the water while you lie here looking like the diva you are and see how many men try to hit on you while I'm gone."

"Are you serious?"

Lynette stood up and slowly backed away from Eve with a teasing grin. "I'll be right back."

❖

"Lynette!" Eve called with a laugh.

She shook her head and grabbed her sunscreen. When a shadow appeared a moment later, she glanced up to find a man standing near the blanket.

He knelt beside her with a toothy grin. "You look like you could use some help with that."

"Excuse me?" Eve said.

"You look like you need some help getting sunscreen on your back. Thought I would offer my services."

Eve held back a laugh. Lynette hadn't been gone for five minutes and this guy was making a play for her.

She gave him a pleasant smile. "Thank you but I'm good."

Unfortunately, he didn't take the hint and boldly sat down on the blanket.

"So, are you and your friend here alone?"

"Not exactly, we're here together."

"My friends and I are renting a house nearby. Why don't you both join us later for a little get-together?"

Eve gave the man a visual once-over. He was young, good-looking, and physically fit. Paige would call him perfect boy-toy material, especially since he seemed so confident in his game. She glanced toward the water and saw Lynette helping a little boy with a bucket of sand. She'd taken off her T-shirt and wore a bikini top with her surfer shorts. Her dark skin glistened from the water and her vibrant joy for life showed in her smile. It made Eve's heart flutter in her chest.

She turned back to the man beside her. "Thanks for the offer, but hanging out with a room full of strangers isn't really how I had planned on spending a first date."

He looked confused and Eve thought she would have to completely spell out the word *lesbian* before he figured out what she was telling him. Suddenly, a look of comprehension, and then surprise, came over his face.

"You mean you two?" He pointed toward the other chair on the blanket as if Lynette sat on it.

"Are dating? Yes," Eve answered without hesitation.

He shook his head, looking disappointed. "Why would a fine woman like you want to waste all of that sexiness on another woman?"

"This conversation is over. I think you better leave." She had tried to be nice, but this guy was obviously too full of himself to even notice that she wasn't the least bit interested in him.

"Maybe you just haven't found a man to give it to you the right way," he said with a cocky grin.

"Oh, and you think you can be that man?"

"I haven't had any complaints yet." He reached toward her and ran a finger along her forearm.

Eve swatted his hand away as if he were a worrisome insect. "Tell me something, why do men think that all lesbians need is a good man and they'll be all right? For your information, I've had a good man, several good men as a matter of fact, and none of them could even imagine giving me the satisfaction a woman could, in or out of the bed. So, take your game somewhere else."

With a disgusted suck of his teeth, he stood. "Your loss," he said with a shrug before walking away.

Eve laughed out loud. "Unbelievable."

"What did I miss?" Lynette asked, glancing at the retreating figure then looking curiously at Eve.

Still chuckling, Eve explained what happened.

Lynette's eyes widened in surprise. "You actually told him we were dating?"

"Yes." It dawned on Eve what the implication of that meant.

Lynette sat down beside her. "And what you said about no man ever satisfying you like a woman could, did you mean it or were you just trying to get him to leave?"

Eve met Lynette's dark gaze with a smile. "I meant it."

Lynette grinned broadly. "Wow."

"I don't know what's happening, but I'm finding that being around or talking to you has me admitting to things I haven't said to anyone."

"Is that so bad?"

"No. I like that I can be so open with you. It's something I haven't been able to do with anyone."

"Not even Paige?"

"We've been best friends for over twenty years, yet I never really felt confident enough to truly be myself around her. I've been hiding the truth for so long I guess I was too afraid of being myself…"

"…because someone would see the truth," Lynette finished.

"Yeah, I guess so. Was it like that for you?"

"Pretty much, although I came out my senior year in high school because I eventually got tired of living my mother's lies. When people started questioning my sexuality because of the way I preferred to dress or my mannerisms, she would tell them I was just a tomboy and would eventually grow out of it. I even dated a few guys just to appease her." Lynette chuckled. "Funny thing was the guys I dated were just as much in the closet as I was."

"You told me your mother is a very devout Christian. How did she take it when you finally told her?"

The sadness and hurt from that day still felt fresh. "She was hurt, but surprisingly it had nothing to do with her faith. She blamed it on her parenting because she'd allowed my tomboyish ways to go on too long."

"Really?"

"Yeah. It was like that for a few years before I convinced her to go to a Parents, Families, and Friends of Lesbians and Gays meeting with me. After talking to other parents, she finally stopped blaming herself. She's now regularly active with the chapter in Queens."

"You're lucky to have such understanding parents. I can't imagine mine wanting to hear me admit to being gay, let alone going to a meeting with other parents to talk about it."

"I only have one understanding parent. My father refuses to discuss it," Lynette said with a sigh.

Eve reached over and took Lynette's hand, in what she assumed was supposed to be a comforting gesture, but something passed between them that sent a spark of desire from their clasped hands throughout her body.

Eve cleared her throat nervously. "Why don't we have lunch." She gently removed her hand from Lynette's.

"Good idea." Lynette said, knowing food wouldn't appease the hunger she was feeling. "Can I help with anything?" she asked as Eve took out several containers of Tupperware from the cooler she'd brought.

"No, you just sit back and enjoy."

Lynette did as she was told and sat back in her beach chair, stretched out her legs, and folded her hands in her lap as she watched Eve. The fluid, graceful way she moved, the way her thick, curly hair brushed across her shoulders and back, the curve of her waist, the roundness of her hips, her smooth feet and manicured toes, Lynette watched all of that with an appreciative eye. Eve passed Lynette a plate, and she didn't miss how Eve's hand trembled as she did. They ate their lunch quietly, surreptitiously glancing at one another while Lynette tried hard to ignore the sexual tension floating between them. She didn't know how she managed to make it through the afternoon without pulling Eve into her arms and seducing her right on the beach, but she did. She wasn't so sure that would be the case after they left. Eve brought out a need Lynette hadn't experienced in quite some time.

❖

Lynette had arranged for them to use a friend's beach condo in the area to shower and change for a wine tasting and dinner at a local winery.

"This is nice," Eve commented when they walked into the cozy one-bedroom apartment.

"Yeah, my friend uses it when things get hectic and she needs to get out of the city. Why don't you go ahead and use the bathroom first? It opens up to the bedroom as well, so you'll have some privacy," Lynette offered.

"Thank you. I won't be long."

Lynette watched the sway of Eve's hips as she walked. Once the bathroom door closed, she shook her head, sighed, and then went to the kitchen hoping her friend had left some beer in the refrigerator. After grabbing one, she opened it and took a large swig, hoping to clear the fog clouding her mind. The intensity of her attraction to Eve had her worried. It was too easy, too comfortable, as if they'd known each other much longer. They'd only gone out twice and Lynette was itching to walk into the bathroom to join Eve in the shower. She went over to the door but didn't turn the knob, just listened to the splash of the water, the scrape of the shower door opening and closing, and the softness of Eve's voice as she began humming a tune.

Lynette laid her forehead against the door, closed her eyes, and let her imagination run. Playing like a movie in her mind's eye was the erotic image of Eve's voluptuous curves through the steam of the shower. She could see Eve gently soaping her body, running her hands slowly down her neck, across her shoulders, down her chest, cupping her breast, then sliding down her softly rounded belly, working her way lower to her hips and eventually the treasure lying at the juncture of her thighs. Lynette refused to allow her imagination to go any further. If she did there would be no stopping her from making a big mistake. She forced herself away from the door, grabbed another beer from the refrigerator, and walked out to the patio.

❖

After showering and dressing, Eve came out to an empty living room. Noticing the open glass doors, she walked out onto the patio to find Lynette standing at the edge of the shoreline, staring out at the horizon with a beer bottle in her hand. As if sensing Eve's presence, she turned and smiled, plodding her way through the sand toward her, then climbing the steps to stand beside her.

Eve sighed in contentment. "This is so peaceful. I could see why your friend likes to come here to escape. I'd never want to leave."

"We could always stay and get something delivered," Lynette suggested.

Eve glanced over at her with a smile. "Too tipsy to drive?" she teased her.

"Yes, but not from the beer."

Her dark, heated gaze drew Eve to her. Their heads moved toward each other in unison. The kiss was slow, soft, and gentle, only lasting for a moment yet leaving a very lasting impression. They rested their foreheads against one another.

Lynette slowly stepped away. "I better go shower and change."

Eve gazed at her through a haze of desire. "What about that offer to stay in?"

Lynette grinned knowingly. "That might not be such a good idea."

"Yeah, I guess it wouldn't," Eve grudgingly admitted.

Lynette was quicker to shower and change than Eve had been, but that didn't mean she looked any less hot. Eve suddenly felt as if she'd forgotten how to breathe as Lynette walked out of the bedroom adjusting the cuff of her suit jacket. She wore a teal plaid suit with cuffed cigarette pants, a lavender button-down shirt, lavender and plaid pocket square, and brown lace-up ankle boots. The textured waves in her hair glistened with whatever product she used, and the most intoxicating cologne drifted toward Eve, wreaking havoc with her senses. It took her a moment to realize Lynette was speaking to her.

"Huh?"

Lynette grinned knowingly. "Are you ready to go?"

Eve felt her face heat in embarrassment. "Uh, yes. Let me just make sure I have everything."

She rushed past Lynette toward the bedroom to not only grab her bag but to get herself together. Both times she had seen Lynette prior to tonight she'd been dressed somewhat casually but still looking good. Seeing her dressed so elegantly and smelling so delicious had Eve's body temperature rising by several degrees and left her aching with desire. She focused on making sure everything she'd brought with her was in her bag, even though she had already done that after she'd gotten dressed. It gave her time to calm her body down before she faced Lynette again, although the fact that whatever cologne she had used still filled the room with its seductive scent didn't help. A few minutes later, Eve had managed to calm down enough to act somewhat normal.

"Okay, ready whenever you are," she said with a smile.

"Great. Let me take that for you," Lynette said, reaching for Eve's bag.

Their fingers brushed as Eve handed it over and her body went into overdrive from the innocent touch. She said, "Thank you," but it sounded too breathy to even be considered words.

They both stood gazing at each other as if hesitant to leave.

Lynette's eyes were a dark ebony as she looked at Eve. "If you tell me you want to stay, I'll have no objections."

Eve's body was screaming "STAY" before Lynette even finished the sentence, but her heart and mind won out. The moment she and Stefan decided to divorce, she had decided that when she was ready to start dating again, it would be with women. She had also decided that she would take her time before rushing into anything, intimately and emotionally. She needed her heart to be just as ready as her body because once she made that decision, telling her family would shortly follow, and she wasn't quite ready for that.

"As tempting as the offer sounds, I think going out to dinner is the best idea."

Lynette gave her a sexy smile and nodded. "Okay."

❖

Dinner was at a restaurant run by a local winery. Since she was driving, Lynette chose to drink water but insisted Eve enjoy herself and order whatever she liked.

"Are you sure? I feel like a lush drinking alone."

Lynette quirked a brow. "Did you think I would bring you to a winery-owned restaurant and not expect you to drink wine?"

Eve grinned. "I guess not."

They discussed the menu, Lynette made some recommendations along with wine pairings since she had been to the restaurant on several occasions, and then they placed their order.

"This afternoon was fun," Eve said.

"It was. I can't remember the last time I built a sandcastle."

"Well, you're very good at it and I think that mom appreciated you keeping her children occupied while she was trying to feed her baby."

"Yeah, I saw her struggling and couldn't help but give her a hand. Besides, I love kids."

"Do you want any of your own?" Eve asked.

Lynette smiled broadly. "Yeah, I wouldn't mind having a couple of rug rats to call my own. What about you?"

"Same. Stefan and I tried but we couldn't conceive. Medically, we were both fine. I guess it just wasn't meant to be."

Lynette reached across the table and placed her hand over Eve's. "I'm sorry."

"I'm not. If we had children, it would've made leaving more difficult."

They hadn't discussed children during their previous lengthy calls, and Lynette wasn't sure if it was too soon to discuss the topic, but since Eve brought it up she was happy to hear they agreed on the subject.

"My mother is a big believer of everything happening for a reason."

Eve gave her a small smile. "I guess that would include our meeting each other."

"You think so?"

"Yes, at least the timing of it. Since my divorce I've put my romantic life on the back burner to focus on building my business. For the past few months, Paige had been trying to get me to start dating again, but I've been hesitant. I knew I wanted to date women, but getting back into dating after a divorce these days is tough even if I were straight. I've looked at some of these dating apps, and they are not only intimidating but made me feel old and realize how inhibited I am. In the end I just continued using my business as an excuse."

Lynette nodded in understanding. "Dating apps are a lot for the out and proud folks our age. I can only imagine how intimidating they would be for someone still working their way out. I guess Paige not knowing the truth about you also didn't help."

"No, it didn't. As close as we are, there would've been no way for me to actively start dating without her input. She would've insisted on creating my dating profile and screening potential dates herself."

"Well, in a way, she did help you. If it weren't for her, we would've never met and I, for one, am glad she called you," Lynette said, smiling.

Eve's gorgeous smile lit up Lynette's heart. "So am I."

Their first course was brought out, and like their first dinner together just a week before, time got away from them as they talked. It felt so easy to talk to Eve. To freely share her thoughts and opinions and listen as Eve did the same because they were so similar. And when they disagreed on a topic, there was no right or wrong, just mutual respect for each other's differing opinions. By the time they were heading back to the city, Lynette knew her heart was in trouble.

❖

When they arrived at Eve's apartment, Lynette helped her gather her cooler and bag and walked her to the entrance of the building.

Eve turned to Lynette with a smile. "I had a really great time."

"I did too."

"Would you like to come up?"

Lynette hesitated. "Maybe for a minute. I've got an early day tomorrow."

She hoped that excuse would keep her out of trouble. She didn't want to rush into this and mess it up just as it was getting started.

Eve put her bag just inside the door, then took the cooler from Lynette.

"I'll put this in the kitchen. Would you like something to drink?"

"A glass of water would be good."

"Okay, have a seat in the living room. I'll be right back."

As Eve walked away, Lynette's eyes were drawn to the

seductive sway of her hips. Despite the offer she had made earlier that evening to stay at the condo, Lynette had managed to keep her physical reaction to Eve in check. She wasn't sure if she would be able to do it again if the opportunity arose. She walked into the living room determined to only stay for a few minutes. She wasn't sure if she could continue a polite distance much longer than that. Walking toward the sofa, Lynette noticed *Venus's Garden* lying on the coffee table. She picked it up, flipped through the pages, and could see that it had been read often. She smiled broadly at the thought of Eve curled up on the sofa reading her book.

"I forgot I left that there," Eve said, her face flushed with embarrassment as she handed Lynette a glass of water.

Lynette laid the book back on the table. "It's kind of strange to see it sitting on someone's coffee table."

"You're an amazing writer. I can't wait to see what your next project will be."

"Thanks. I've been working on a novel for some time. I'm just not sure if I want to move away from the erotica and poetry into a completely different genre. It may not do as well."

"What's it about?" Eve sat on the sofa, folding her legs beneath her.

Lynette sat beside her. "I'd like to do a series of crime and mystery novels about a female detective."

"Crime novels are always big sellers. Why would you think it wouldn't do as well?"

"Because the main character is gay."

"I don't see that making a difference. You already have a following with your current audience. You should finish it. Besides, who says you can't do both?"

Lynette smiled. "You think so?"

Shrugging, Eve grinned. "Like I said, you're an amazing writer. Even your erotic short stories have more to them than just sex. They have a depth that keeps the reader interested in the characters' stories just as much as the sex."

"You keep talking like that, you're going to make my head swell. I'll have to keep you around for ego boosting."

"Is that a promise?"

Lynette gazed at her curiously.

"Why are you looking at me like that?" Eve asked.

"I'm just wondering if I should leave before I do something that we may both regret in the morning."

Eve's lips turned up into a sexy grin. "Well, if it helps, I don't want you to leave, and if I was worried about regret, I wouldn't have asked you up."

Lynette set her glass on the table, then moved to close the gap between them, gently taking Eve's face in her hands. She intended for the kiss to be a brief taste, but once her lips met the soft fullness of Eve's, all her good intentions flew right out the window. Lynette had been holding back her passion for this woman all day, but when Eve wrapped her arms around her waist and her soft curves fell against Lynette's body, there was no closing the floodgate as it all burst forth.

❖

Eve felt as if she were being consumed by a fire that burned from within. It began where their lips met, then spread throughout her body with a raging force. Lynette moved her hands from Eve's face up to the neatly secured bun at the nape of her neck, releasing the clip that held the thick locks in place and burying her fingers in Eve's hair. Eve moaned into Lynette's mouth, pulling their bodies flush against one another to deepen the kiss. That little voice of reason in Eve's head screamed that this was happening too fast, but her lust-filled body betrayed her. The feel of Lynette's soft hands along her body and firm breasts pressed against her own was too much for Eve to resist.

Lynette eased her lips from Eve's to kiss her way down her neck. Eve didn't know how, but one minute she and Lynette were sitting and the next she was lying under Lynette, her head thrown back and breasts heaving from the cleavage of her dress. Lynette sat up just enough to unbutton the front of Eve's dress, spreading the material open, and gazing hungrily at her.

"No one's ever looked at me the way you do. It's like you're touching me without laying a finger on me," Eve said softly.

Lynette grinned. "I could look at you all night."

Eve quirked a brow. "If you're going to be here all night, I would hope you would do more than look."

Lynette lowered her head. "You mean something like this?" She swirled the tip of her tongue around Eve's navel, then along her belly where the waistband of her panties began.

"Mmm." Eve's hips rose off the sofa.

Her moans grew as the heat of Lynette's mouth burned her skin through the lacy fabric of her underwear, trailing a path toward the vee at the juncture of her thighs. Writhing beneath Lynette's intimate kisses, Eve ran her hands over Lynette's lowered head, enjoying the soft waves of her hair.

Halting her descent, Lynette gazed up at Eve. "I want to taste you, Eve," she whispered.

Eve met her gaze, nodding in response. She no longer cared that they'd only met a few weeks ago, that it was probably too soon to be taking this step, she just knew that she wanted Lynette more than she'd ever wanted anyone before.

❖

Lynette grasped the waistband of Eve's sheer black lace low-rise briefs that matched her bra and had Eve looking like a delicately decorated sweet laid out for her enjoyment and slowly eased them down her rounded hips and shapely legs. Lynette knelt on the floor, gently shifted Eve's hips, spread her legs, and placed a soft kiss on the neatly trimmed, downy hair of her vagina. Lynette darted the tip of her tongue in and out, teasing and tasting Eve before slowly sliding it up and down her now damp and swollen lips and clit.

Lynette moaned deeply in her throat as Eve's womanly nectar began to flow over her tongue. She licked, sucked, and explored Eve hungrily, her own excitement building over the sweet taste of the beautiful woman beneath her. Eve grasped Lynette's head, frantically pumping her hips toward her face as her steady pants of breath turned into a low keening. Lynette could feel the boxer briefs she wore becoming damp in response.

❖

So caught up in the mind-blowing pleasure Lynette was giving her, Eve barely heard her phone buzzing on the table. She wouldn't have been able to answer it anyway because Lynette's fingers joined in the play, and the combination of tongue, lips, and fingers was too much. Eve's body was flooded with the most intense sensations, and she let out a series of high-pitched "Ohs" that she was sure the entire building heard, but she didn't care. Afterward, Lynette's head rested against Eve's thigh as they both tried to calm their heavy breathing.

"Are you all right?" Eve asked in a hoarse whisper.

Lynette chuckled. "Most definitely. What about you?"

Eve smiled in satisfaction. "Oh, I'm fine."

Lynette laughed and moved to sit on the couch beside her.

Eve shifted so that she could curl up against her. As soon as they were settled, her phone buzzed again.

"Someone seems determined to talk to you," Lynette said.

With a frustrated sigh, Eve reached for her phone, but by the time she answered, the call had gone to voice mail and her mother's name popped up on the screen as a missed call. Eve sat up, and in her rush to listen to the voice mail, she swiped the speakerphone as well.

"Hey, Eve, it's Mommy. I guess you're busy. I talked to Tony today and he said he thinks you're seeing someone. Why wouldn't you tell me? Anyway, if you don't get in too late, give me a call. Te quiero."

Eve tensed, eased away from Lynette, stood, and quickly began buttoning her dress.

"Fuck." She barely heard Lynette say under her breath as she stood as well. "I'm going to go." She headed for the door without a backward glance at Eve.

"What? Wait. Why are you leaving?" Eve asked in confusion.

"I've got an early day tomorrow." Lynette's tone was tense.

Eve's thoughts ran quickly through her mind as she tried to figure out why Lynette was suddenly so cold, but she couldn't find a reason for the change.

"So that's it? Wine me, dine me, lick me, and leave me. Is that how you do it?" Eve said angrily.

Lynette turned to her with a confused gaze. "You don't want me to leave?"

"No. Why would you think that?"

"Because you seemed in a real big hurry to get away from me after hearing your mother's message."

"I wasn't in a hurry to get away from you. I got freaked out by my mother saying that my brother Tony told her I was seeing someone. The only person I had talked to about seeing you was Paige, who's married to Tony. Paige promised me she wouldn't say anything to my family until I was ready to tell them."

"Oh," Lynette said, looking embarrassed.

Eve walked over, then gently took Lynette's face in her hands. "Lynette, I'm very much attracted to you and not the least bit ashamed of it. Most of all, I'm not Marisol and won't do to you what she did."

Lynette pulled Eve into her arms. "You asked me once to be patient with your coming out, now I have to ask the same of you with my doubts after Marisol. I guess I'm not completely over what happened."

"I'm going to have to prove not all of us partially closeted women are alike."

Lynette hugged Eve tighter. "You don't have to prove anything to me."

Eve pulled away just enough to look into Lynette's eyes. "I'm glad to hear that."

Lynette smiled. "You should go call your mother, and I really do have an early day tomorrow."

Eve nodded. "Okay."

"I know I probably don't deserve it after how I just acted, but do I get a kiss good night?"

Eve acted as if she was seriously considering whether to do it, then smiled. "I guess so."

Without her heels, Eve was much shorter than Lynette. She stood on tiptoe, and Lynette met her halfway. The kiss was softer, more tender than the passionate ones they'd shared moments before.

"I'll call you tomorrow," Lynette said.

"Okay."

Lynette gave Eve one last peck before leaving.

Eve locked the door behind her, standing with her back against it for a few moments as she closed her eyes to remember the passion Lynette had given her. She hadn't felt true passion for someone in so long she'd forgotten what it was like. She just hoped her fear of her family's reaction to her coming out and Lynette's fear of being rejected wouldn't get in the way of what could be a wonderful relationship.

CHAPTER FOUR

Eve decided to wait until morning to speak with Paige and her mother. It was after ten o'clock by the time Lynette left, and she wasn't ready for a conversation with her mother after the intimate experience they'd just shared. She wanted to go to sleep with the afterglow from their moment fresh on her mind and body. Her dreams were filled with Lynette's long fingers, soft lips, and strong tongue doing things to her body she'd never thought possible. The dreams were so vivid she woke up breathing heavily and covered in sweat. Sighing, she glanced over at her alarm clock. It was a little past six in the morning. She normally started her day at seven, so it made no sense trying to go back to sleep. Instead, she showered, made herself a cup of tea, and then went to her office to get some work done. About an hour later, her phone rang. Who could possibly be calling her this early in the morning? She frowned when she saw Paige's name.

"You know I'm going to kick your ass when I see you," Eve greeted Paige.

"Aw hell, Mom Monroe called you, didn't she? I was hoping I'd get to you before she did."

"I thought we had an agreement."

"We do. You know after all these years I'm not gonna betray you."

"Then explain to me how my brother, your husband, knows I'm seeing someone?"

Eve heard Paige sigh. "Are you gonna give me a chance to explain?"

"Make it fast," Eve said in annoyance.

"Tony overheard me talking to you about your plans for your date. I didn't know it until I heard him telling your mother about our conversation. Fortunately, he didn't hear me say a name, so he has no clue it's a woman."

Relief flooded through Eve. "I guess I won't kick your ass after all."

Paige chuckled. "You wouldn't even know how."

"Whatever. You're sure Tony has no idea about Lynette?"

"Positive. After I cursed him out for listening in on my phone conversation, I asked him how much he heard. It was just enough to hear where you were going. What did your mother say?"

Eve told Paige the message her mother left. "I'm going to see her this afternoon."

"Are you gonna to tell her?"

"I don't know. I don't think I'm quite ready for that."

"Well, you know if you need backup, I'll be there," Paige offered.

"I know." Eve was glad she had such an understanding friend.

"So, how did everything go yesterday?"

"It was nice."

"Nice?" Paige said doubtfully.

Eve grinned. "Okay, it was very nice." Eve told her about their day, purposely leaving out what happened after they returned to her apartment. That was a detail Paige didn't need to hear.

"You mean to tell me you spent an entire day with a woman

who writes some of the hottest erotic stories I've ever read, and she didn't even try and kiss you?" Paige said in disbelief.

"Yes, she did, but she also treated me with the utmost respect."

For a moment, Eve only heard silence on the other end of the line. "You're really falling for her, aren't you?" Paige finally said.

"I didn't say that."

"Eve, I've known you far too long not to be able to tell when you're falling. From what I hear in your voice, you're about to hit the ground any second."

"You make it sound like that's a bad thing."

"It is if Lynette's not there to catch you. Is she?"

Eve smiled, remembering last night. "She hasn't actually said it, but I think she is."

"Well, try to hold yourself up until you find out."

"Paige, you worry too much. This is the first time I've gone on a date for over a year. Let me just enjoy it, okay?"

"I worry because I love you."

Eve smiled affectionately. "I know."

"Call me later to let me know how your conversation with Mom Monroe went."

"Okay."

Eve hung up wondering if Paige was right. Was she falling for Lynette too quickly? Was she reading too much into a physical attraction because she'd been lonely for so long? She enjoyed the easy vibe she and Lynette shared. How Lynette treated her during their day together showed that she enjoyed it just as much as Eve did. Remembering the passion in Lynette's gaze was enough to have Eve pushing the doubts Paige put in her head to the back of her mind.

That afternoon, Eve stood on the doorstep of the brownstone she'd grown up in wondering if she should've just called her mother rather than see her in person. It was much easier to lie over the phone. As she'd ridden the subway from Manhattan to Brooklyn, Eve thought it would be best just to be honest with her mother, but the disappointment she knew she'd see in her mother's eyes was just too much to even think about.

Eve still had a key, so she let herself in. "*Hola*, Mommy," she called.

"Eve! What a surprise. I'm in the kitchen."

As Eve walked in the direction of the kitchen, a familiar aroma drifted toward her. She found her mother stirring something in a large pot on the stove.

Eve smiled broadly. "Mmm…you made your paella."

"You know it's your father's favorite." Turning away from the stove, her mother smiled and opened her arms.

Eve stepped into her embrace, breathing in her signature vanilla scent and feeling all the warmth and comfort a mother's arms could bring a troubled child.

"How's Daddy?"

"Good, he and your brothers are still working on that house in Jersey."

"Really? I thought they finished that project last week?"

Eve's father and brothers owned a residential construction business.

"So did your father, but the owner made some last-minute changes. So, what brings you for a visit in the middle of the afternoon?"

"I was going to be in the area, so I decided to stop in and see you." Let the lies begin, Eve thought guiltily.

Her mother gazed at her doubtfully. "Really?"

"You don't believe me?"

"I didn't say that. I know some of the vendors you work

with are in Brooklyn, but as often as you're here you've never just dropped in."

Smiling, Eve shook her head thinking this was why she should've just called. Pilar Monroe may have been able to pass for Eve's older sister, but she had a wizened mother's instinct.

"I got your message last night and thought it would be nice to talk in person instead of over the phone."

"Okay. Let's go sit and chat." Eve's mother looped her arm through hers as they made their way to the living room.

"Oh, by the way, I ran into Stefan the other day," her mother announced.

"Really? Where?"

"At the senior center when I dropped our neighbor, Mrs. Ford, off for her weekly card game."

Eve shrugged. "That's not a surprise. I know he still does volunteer work at quite a few senior facilities."

"Well, I don't think this visit had anything to do with volunteer work. He was picking up a nurse who works there. It seems they've been seeing each other for a few months now."

"He told you this?"

"No. He told me he was picking up a friend, then we chatted about how the practice is doing. One of the other nurses I asked told me the rest." Her mother grinned mischievously.

Eve chuckled. "Mommy, you're a mess. Does he seem happy?"

"From what I could tell by the smile on his face when his 'friend' came out, I think so. Why? Are you having regrets?"

"No, not at all, I think he deserves to be happy and it's good that he's dating someone else in the medical field. I don't think I was a particularly good doctor's wife," Eve said with a small smile.

Neither Stefan's nor her family knew the truth of why

their marriage ended. They agreed to tell everyone that things had become strained between them trying to run the practice and that they thought it would be best to end things before it became too contentious. Fortunately, both families knew how dedicated Stefan was to his work and didn't question it.

"He's not the only one who deserves to be happy," her mother said. "Your father and I have been worried that you spend more time organizing other people's weddings, baby showers, and life-changing events than making time for your own."

"Well, there's no need to worry. I'm fine."

"I'm sure you are, but you can also find some time to have fun."

Eve sighed. "You sound like Paige."

"Speaking of Paige, why do I have to hear from your nosy brother that you're dating someone?"

This was it, Eve thought. She was hoping to get through this part of their conversation quickly so that she wouldn't have to reveal too much.

"It was only one date. I didn't know how it would go, so it didn't make sense telling you guys about it. Since the divorce, the first thing you all ask when you talk to me is if I'm seeing anyone. If I told you I was interested in someone, you'd have us married off by the end of the week."

Eve's mother chuckled. "We're not that bad."

Eve grinned. "No, but you're close. Tony, Miguel, Alex, and Chris are always trying to fix me up with someone they know, and if you and Daddy see me just talking to a man, your faces light up like a Christmas tree."

"We just want you to be happy."

Eve took her mother's hand. "I know, Mommy, and I am happy. I like where I am in my life right now. There's no pressure. I'm free to concentrate on my business, enjoy a quiet night at home, or maybe go on a date if someone of interest does come along."

Her mother gave her a knowing grin. "In other words, we need to mind our own business."

Eve laughed. "In so many words, yes."

"Well, may I at least ask about this person you spent the entire day with?"

"Yes." Eve tried to keep a neutral look on her face despite her nervousness.

"Where did you meet?"

"At an event I did for Paige's agency a few weeks ago."

"A few weeks ago? What took him so long to ask you out?"

"We had scheduling conflicts, but we talked on the phone quite a bit before our date yesterday."

"He must have made quite an impression for you to have spent the entire day with him. Tony said you had plans to go to the Hamptons. Did you have a good time?"

Eve would strangle Tony the next time she saw him. "Yes. It was nice."

Eve's mother gazed at her curiously. "You know when you first met Stefan you couldn't stop talking about him. Now getting information from you about a man you spent an entire day with is like pulling teeth. What's really going on, Eve?"

Eve put on her best smile. "Nothing. It was just a date. Now," she stood to leave before she accidentally said too much, "I have to get to a meeting. I just wanted to come by and see you."

Eve could practically see her mother's mind trying to come up with something that would explain her strange behavior, but she knew the truth was far from what her mother would imagine.

"You know you can talk to me, *hija*."

Eve hugged her mother tightly, "I know, Mommy, but there's nothing going on right now to talk about." Another lie. If she kept this up, she was going to have to go to confession soon. "I promise to call you when there is."

"I'm going to hold you to that." Her mother gave her an understanding smile.

As much as Eve hated lying to her mother, she just wasn't ready to be so open about what was really going on in her life. Her aunt and many of the family in Puerto Rico hadn't been the only ones to turn their backs on Julian. Her mother had taken Aunt Cecilia's side when Julian tried to reconnect with the family and been turned away. Even her brother Tony, who had been close with Julian, refused to talk to or about what happened. No, Eve thought, there was no way she was ready to talk to anyone but Paige about Lynette.

❖

"Lynette…Earth to Lynette…What's going on with you?"

Lynette shook her head. "I'm sorry, Michelle. I guess I'm a little distracted."

"A little. You've barely heard a word I've said since we sat down. Who is she?"

Lynette chuckled at her sister's knowing grin. "Is it that obvious?"

"Only to someone who knows you as well as I do."

Lynette's sister, Michelle, had been the first person she'd come out to and who'd sat beside her when she came out to their parents and brother. She wasn't just Lynette's sister but her best friend and confidante.

"Do you remember the event planner for my book launch?"

"Yeah, the sexy little number in the great shoes I wanted."

Lynette smiled. "Yeah, that one. Her name is Eve."

"I thought I caught you making googly-eyes at her a few times during the night," Michelle teased.

"Googly-eyes?"

Michelle shrugged. "That's what happens when you spend so much time talking to a seven-year-old."

"Don't blame my nephew for your lack of vocabulary. Anyway, you're right. I could barely keep my eyes off her, so I asked her out."

"When did this happen? You usually tell me when you meet someone you actually feel is worth going on a date with."

"There were some things I had to be sure of before I told you anything."

"She's not out, is she?" It was more a statement than a question.

Lynette could hear the worry in her sister's tone. After witnessing everything Lynette had gone through with Marisol, Michelle made it her personal crusade to ensure she wouldn't go through it again. Lynette could barely talk to a woman when Michelle was around because she'd jump in and give the woman the third degree, scaring her off before any real conversation could happen.

"I told you I wasn't dating women who weren't open about their sexuality."

"That doesn't answer my question," Michelle said with a raised brow.

With a sigh of resignation, Lynette looked away, not wanting to see the disappointment she knew would be in her sister's eyes. "Not completely."

"Lynette, why would you put yourself through that again? Wasn't what Marisol did enough to show you that getting involved with a woman like that only leads to heartache?"

"Eve is nothing like Marisol. Her attraction to women is

more than just a result of a marriage that ended badly. As a matter of fact, her marriage ended because she couldn't keep lying to herself or her ex-husband about her sexuality. She came out to him before their divorce and recently came out to her best friend," Lynette explained knowing that probably wouldn't be good enough for her sister but hoping it would appease her for now.

Michelle was quiet for a moment. "When do I get to meet her?"

"Don't you mean when do you get to interrogate her?"

Michelle grinned mischievously. "If she's secure in who she is, a few little questions shouldn't scare her off."

Lynette snorted. "Yeah, right. I think I'll give it a little more time before I throw her in the lion's den."

Michelle gazed at her curiously. "Wow, she must be something."

Lynette grinned as memories of the day she and Eve spent together ran across her mind. "Yeah, she is."

After lunch with her sister, Lynette called Eve. She was a little disappointed when her voice mail picked up, but just hearing Eve's soft, sexy voice in the message was enough to bring a smile.

"Hi, it's Lynette. I just wanted to let you know I was thinking about you. Hope your conversation with your mom went well. Give me a call if you're not too busy. Bye."

Lynette chuckled to herself. She knew she was hooked now. She'd never called a woman just to say she was thinking about them. Eve's natural sexiness, voluptuous figure, and outgoing personality reminded Lynette of her best friend from high school. Toni Lawrence had transferred from another school their junior year, and she and Lynette had hit it off from day one. Toni was very much into her boyfriend of three years, so Lynette knew they would never be more than friends, but it didn't stop her from wishing for more.

Toni seemed clueless about Lynette's longing stares or how often she found a reason to touch Toni in some way or another. Whenever Lynette slept over at her house, Toni would parade around the bedroom in just her bra and panties, her full, voluptuous curves awakening desires Lynette tried so hard to fight, but she endured it just so that she could be with her. There were times when Toni would look at her and Lynette swore that she knew the effect she had on her, but Lynette was too afraid of losing their friendship to say anything.

They went on that way for two years with Lynette suffering in silence until a few nights before they left for college.

❖

Toni suggested they have one last sleepover before they went their separate ways. Lynette had recently come out to her family and decided that would be the night she'd break the news to Toni. As they got ready for bed, Toni changed her usual routine of coming out of the bathroom dressed in just a bra and panties by coming out completely naked. Lynette was too shocked to say or do anything but stare. Toni walked slowly toward her, wrapped her arms around Lynette's neck, and kissed her soundly on the mouth. Lynette came to her senses when she felt Toni's tongue trying to ease between her lips. She took Toni's arms from around her neck and stepped away from her.

"What are you doing?" Lynette asked, reason warring with the arousal coursing through her body.

Toni gazed at Lynette knowingly. "You don't think, after all this time, I haven't noticed the way you look at me or how you find excuses to touch me? Why do you think I come out here barely dressed whenever you spend the night? But I guess you're just too nice to make the first move, which goes to show how loyal a friend you are and why I'm making the move now."

Lynette started to deny it, but Toni knew her too well. "What about Dante?" she asked, reaching for a last-ditch effort to stop this before it went any further.

Toni cupped Lynette's cheek and placed a soft kiss on her lips. "This isn't about Dante. It's about you and me."

Lynette's mind tried to rationalize why what Toni wanted couldn't happen, but years of wishing and wanting this very thing was too much for her. Toni gave herself fully and completely to Lynette that night and well into the next morning when her parents left for work. But it came with a promise that it would stay just between them and be the first and last time they would ever be together that way. Lynette had hesitantly agreed, believing that Toni would eventually change her mind, but she didn't. Toni went off to Penn State and Lynette to Alabama A&M a few days later. Although they kept in touch, Toni refused to talk about what happened that night. The last time Lynette saw Toni was at her wedding shortly after college graduation.

❖

Lynette kept her promise, never telling anyone about that night. She had also never told Toni that prior to that night she had never done more than kiss another girl. Toni had been the first girl she'd made love to. Lynette knew that she would never forget or regret it. After that she'd had brief relationships with other women but never connected with another like she had with Toni until Marisol came along.

Lynette had believed she'd found something different when she and Marisol got together. That she'd finally found a woman she could see herself possibly going the distance with. But her first time in a serious relationship wound up being with a woman who wasn't ready for a serious relationship with her. Now there was Eve, who wasn't out but seemed to be ready for something more than friendship or a brief affair. Lynette felt a wonderful connection with her, but past heartbreak and doubt niggled at the back of her mind.

❖

Eve listened to Lynette's message feeling miserable and only had herself to blame for it. It didn't matter that she'd finally stopped fighting her attraction to women, or that she'd never felt more like herself than she did when she was with Lynette. What mattered was that she couldn't even face her mother with the truth. She was even willing to lie just to avoid disappointing her family.

For the first time in her life, Eve had finally put her wants and needs first and felt guilty as hell about it. Now she was wondering if she was making a mistake with Lynette, who'd been nothing but honest about how what happened with her previous girlfriend affected who she now dated. Because of that, Eve was having doubts about continuing to see Lynette.

In response to Lynette's voice mail, Eve sent her a text message explaining she had meetings all afternoon but would call her this evening. More lies. Something she seemed to be getting quite adept at in such a short time. Then she spent the afternoon throwing herself into paperwork, trying to ignore the battle going on between her head and heart. When the time came, she hesitantly dialed Lynette's number praying her doubts wouldn't ruin what could be something wonderful.

Lynette answered almost immediately. "Hey, great timing, I just walked in the door."

"Do you want to call me back once you get settled?" Eve asked.

"Of course not, I've always got time for you. How was your day?"

"It was okay. I stopped in to see my mother."

"Everything okay? You sound strange."

Eve told Lynette about her conversation with her mother. "Of course, she assumed I had gone out with a man, and I couldn't bring myself to correct her."

"Eve, you just started accepting the truth yourself. No one expects you to suddenly start shouting it to the world."

"How is it I can tell a complete stranger on the beach that I'm dating a woman but can't admit it to my mother?" Eve said in frustration.

"Because a stranger isn't going to judge you the way friends or family will. Telling your family is a big step. Stick with the baby steps. Don't rush yourself before you feel you're ready," Lynette advised her.

"I don't know when I'll ever be ready for that step. My family doesn't have a good history of dealing with something like this."

Eve was met with an achingly long moment of silence on the other end before Lynette said, "I see. So, everything you said last night about knowing what you want, how you want to live didn't mean a thing?" Eve hated the tension she heard in Lynette's voice.

"No, I meant it. I just don't know if my family is ready to accept it."

"You don't know if they're ready to accept IT…or ME?"

"That's not what I meant. You deserve to be with someone

who is ready to be as open and honest with her family about her life as she is with you."

Lynette sighed. "Listen, Eve, I knew what I was getting into after our first dinner together, so what I want or deserve isn't the issue. The issue is that you're afraid of disappointing your family. If you plan on being true to yourself, then it's something you're going to have to deal with at some point. I really feel like we could have something special, but if you feel seeing me is going to make facing your family more difficult, then I don't want to put you in that situation." Disappointment was obvious in her tone.

"Lynette, what are you saying?"

"I'm saying maybe you need some space to figure out what you want because obviously you're not ready for what we could have together," Lynette said.

Eve was so confused. "You said you knew what you were getting into with me. That you wouldn't push me. Now you want to give me space to figure out what I want. Are you sure it's not to give YOU space?"

"I thought I could do this, but I made a promise to myself not to put my heart on the line again for someone who isn't open and ready to do the same. You're not ready, so…" She left the rest unsaid.

Eve wanted to tell Lynette she was wrong, but she wasn't. Eve wasn't ready for what they could have despite knowing that her fear was probably irrational because it was born of something that happened in the past to someone else. That her parents and brothers weren't the same as the Puerto Rico contingent of their family, but the slightest chance that they would have a negative reaction to her revealing her truth kept her from doing so.

"I understand," Eve said miserably.

"I-I'm sorry, Eve. I wish—"

"Bye, Lynette." Eve didn't see any reason to prolong the painful moment.

Lynette was quiet for a moment. "Bye, Eve."

There was a finality to her tone, leaving Eve to wonder if she'd just ruined her chance at the first genuine and honest relationship she'd ever had. The thought of that made her feel extremely lonely.

She'd told her mother that she was happy with her life, but was she? She was doing what she loved. Details by Eve had become so successful that she was looking to hire another planner to help with the overflow. She was no longer in an unhappy marriage and was genuinely pleased to hear that her ex-husband was dating. Finally, she'd been honest with herself by admitting her attraction to women was not just a passing fancy. Yet here she sat, alone and feeling sorry for herself because she was allowing fear to keep her from being with a woman who could possibly help rid her of the loneliness she'd managed to push aside until now.

Eve knew Lynette had doubts about her self-acceptance and she didn't blame her for not wanting to put herself through another episode like what she'd been through with Marisol. With a heavy sigh, Eve typed *counseling for gay women* in her internet search. Although telling her best friend and going on a date with a woman were big steps, they weren't enough for her to walk freely out of the closet into Lynette's arms without being able to deal with the consequences of her decision to do so. She was going to need a helping hand to guide her along the way.

CHAPTER FIVE

The following Sunday, Eve walked through the doors of Identity House filled with anxiety. While she wanted to be able to feel confident about her decision to come out, she still held the fear that she'd lose her family in the process. She wasn't sure anyone would be able to help rid her of that.

"Hi, can I help you?" a young woman cheerfully greeted her.

"That's what I'm here to find out," Eve said with a nervous smile. "My name is Eve Monroe. I'm here to see Nikki."

"Oh, sure, have a seat and I'll give her a buzz."

When Eve did her online search for counseling centers Identity House caught her attention. It seemed fitting since she was going through a serious identity crisis. A quote on their home page seemed to hit her squarely in the chest: *Sometimes, all you need to work through life's challenges is someone to talk to.* It was a simple statement but also very powerful to someone in her situation.

She called and spoke with a woman named Nikki who suggested that Eve come see her at their walk-in peer center. Eve spent the entire week going back and forth with herself about why she shouldn't go and how were a group of strangers who didn't know her family going to be able to help her. Then she remembered how she felt when she was with Lynette and knew she would never have that feeling again if she continued to live this way.

"Eve?"

Hearing her name, Eve turned toward a woman who bore a striking resemblance to her third-grade teacher, Miss Davis. It threw her for a loop because she'd had the biggest crush on the teacher, so it took her a minute to acknowledge the woman.

"Um…yes…I'm Eve."

The woman held out her hand. "Hi, I'm Nikki Sullivan."

Eve took her hand, shaking her head in wonder.

Nikki gazed at her curiously. "Is there something wrong?"

"I apologize. You just look like someone I used to know."

"Well, I hope that's a good thing."

Eve smiled. "It is. She's someone I liked very much."

Nikki chuckled. "That's a relief. Usually when a person says you remind them of someone, it's not a good thing. Let's go to my office and you can tell me what brings you to Identity House."

Eve followed her, still amazed at the resemblance and wondering if this was a sign or just coincidence. She tried not to stare as they walked, but it was difficult.

"Have a seat." Nikki pointed toward a set of chairs then sat in the one across from Eve.

"So, if you don't mind my asking, who's this person I remind you so much of that it's got you all flustered?" Nikki asked.

Eve felt her face heat with a blush. "This is going to sound silly, but you remind me of my third-grade teacher."

Nikki raised an eyebrow. "I know I'm old, but I'm not that old."

Eve's face flushed hotter with embarrassment. "She was young. I think in her mid-thirties."

Nikki chuckled. "Nice recovery. I take it this teacher had quite an effect on your life. I can barely remember what some of my college professors looked like, let alone my third-grade teacher."

Eve smiled at the memory of walking into Miss Davis's class as she greeted each student by name. Her smooth copper complexion glowed, her golden-brown eyes sparkled even under the fluorescent lights, and when she gifted Eve with her bright smile, her eyes crinkled on the sides and dimples appeared in her cheeks making Eve's stomach do little flips.

"I guess she did."

"The first teacher crush," Nikki said knowingly. "I still remember mine, Mrs. Maxwell, English 1A, freshman year of high school."

Eve looked at Nikki curiously. "I didn't say I had a crush on her."

"You didn't have to. It's amazing what a subtle look or blush can tell about a person."

"Is it that obvious?"

"Only to someone who knows what to look for. I studied sociology and human behavior in college. I have a knack for picking up on subtle cues in behavior that most people tend to ignore," Nikki explained.

"Is that why you became a counselor?"

"No, this is volunteer work. My day job is a recruiter for an executive search firm. I volunteer at Identity House because if it weren't for them, I wouldn't be here. I got extremely depressed when I realized I couldn't keep denying, but also couldn't deal with, the truth about my sexuality. Some friends brought me here about ten years ago to keep me from doing something stupid. Now I use my experience and skills to help others work through whatever obstacle is keeping them from being true to themselves."

"That's very commendable."

Shrugging, Nikki grinned. "It's more selfish than commendable. I want everyone who walks through that door to eventually leave here as happy with their own lives as I am with mine. Now, tell me, Eve, what's holding you back?"

Eve liked Nikki's no-nonsense manner. It reminded her of Paige, which made her feel comfortable enough to tell her a condensed version of what was going on in her life. Nikki listened with a quiet attentiveness until Eve finished.

Looking thoughtful for a moment, Nikki asked, "Do you have any gay family members?"

Eve hesitated. "I have a cousin that I haven't seen since I was a little girl when we used to visit family in Puerto Rico every summer. His name was Julian, and I remember him having a huge Barbie doll collection that he'd let me play with when we visited. One year my mother's sister Cecilia, Julian's mother, told us he'd moved out. After that I didn't see him at any family events. Eventually, they started talking about him in the past tense. When I asked my mother about it, she told me he was fine and that I was too young to understand what happened." Eve hadn't believed her, but she didn't question it since it seemed to upset her aunt if anyone did.

"Then I remember, right before I went to high school, going back for his sister Elena's wedding. I was watching my mother and aunts help her get ready when this woman walked into the room who could've been Elena's twin. Elena ran to her and hugged her while the other women stared in shock. My aunt Cecilia finally stood up and started screaming at the woman to leave and that she wasn't welcome in their home. It took both my mother and their two other sisters to calm Cecilia down. Elena begged her mother to let the woman stay but she refused. The woman told Elena it was all right, that she loved her, and then turned to leave. Before she walked out of the room, she spotted me sitting in the corner, smiled, and said, 'Is that you, Evangeline? I would've never recognized you if it weren't for that thick wild hair of yours. You're a little beauty. I bet you're too big to play with Barbies now, aren't you?' That's when I realized that the reason the tall, beautiful woman was causing such a commotion was because she was my cousin Julian, who was now going by Juliana."

"Wow. What was going through your head at the time?" Nikki asked.

"That's the funny thing. I didn't understand what all the fuss was about. It seemed right. Juliana had never seemed comfortable with being a boy. While all the boys were outside running around, getting dirty, playing sports, Juliana was in the house with the girls looking at clothes, playing with dolls, and doing our hair and nails. She was always one of the girls to me even before I understood what that meant. It seems the only ones who didn't have a problem with it were her sister Elena and me. She'd invited her to the wedding hoping to bring her back into the family, but Aunt Cecelia refused to hear it. She said she was a disgrace to the family and that the way she was living was sinful. When Elena asked my mother and our other aunts to help make her mother see how wrong she was, they refused to get involved."

Eve felt an overwhelming sadness at the memory. "My mother's silence was the biggest surprise for me because she was the only one of her sisters who'd left Puerto Rico. She was the most liberal of them all. I thought she'd surely stand up for Juliana, but she didn't. She looked just as ashamed of the situation as her sisters were."

"Has Juliana been accepted back into the family yet?"

"No. Elena told me years later that at the time she was going through the pre-op requirements for her transition. When Aunt Cecelia heard she'd gone through with the surgery, she got rid of everything that had to do with her and said that her son died the day he walked out of her house. Last I heard Juliana is living in Miami and owns a spa."

Nikki gazed at Eve curiously. "You almost sound jealous."

Eve started to deny it but knew it would be a lie. "I guess I am. Despite most of the family's refusal to acknowledge her, she sacrificed everything to become the person she is today, but I can't find the nerve to tell them about my sexuality," she said in frustration.

"Do you think that's because you're worried your mother will have the same reaction as your aunt? That what happened between Cecelia and Juliana will happen with you two?"

Tears blurred Eve's vision as she nodded in response. Nikki moved to the edge of her chair, reaching across the short distance between them to grasp Eve's hand.

"I can't guarantee that won't happen. What I can guarantee is that if you continue trying to balance the good little Catholic daughter who wants to please her mother and the closeted bisexual woman trying to live and love in secret, you're going to tear yourself apart. I know because I was that woman. Sooner or later, something is going to have to give. You can't be everything to everybody, Eve. If you're not true to yourself, you'll never be happy."

Eve knew Nikki was right, but the fear was still there. The fear that her mother would do the same thing Aunt Cecelia did to Juliana, treat her as if she'd never existed.

Nikki reached for a box of Kleenex she kept on a table nearby and handed it to Eve. "Can I make a suggestion?"

Wiping tears from her face, Eve nodded.

"Talk to Juliana. I think that it might help you in understanding what you need to do."

Eve gazed doubtfully at Nikki. "That's easier said than

done. I haven't seen her since Elena's wedding. I don't think calling about this would be the best way to reunite."

"I have a feeling that she may be more understanding than you think. Promise me you'll think about it."

"I'll think about it," Eve said grudgingly.

"I also think it might do you some good to come to a group session. Sometimes hearing that others are experiencing the same issues can help us work through our own."

Nikki took a pamphlet and business card from her desk and handed it to Eve. "That's got my personal cell on it. Don't hesitate to call me if you need to talk. Day or night," she said with an encouraging smile. "If you're not ready for group I'm here next Sunday, same time, same place. I can also get you references to some incredibly good therapists if you need a little more in-depth counseling."

"Thank you, Nikki. It helped just to be able to talk to someone."

"But not enough to decide to talk to your mother anytime soon," Nikki said knowingly.

Eve gave her a sad smile. "Not right now."

"Understandable, although when tough issues arise many women tend to overthink, causing more stress than they're already feeling. The one thing we utilize more than men is our intuition and heart. Listen to your heart, Eve. In the past couple of years, you've followed it, and look where it's led you. You're working in a career you love, you're out of an unhappy marriage, and you have the chance to be in a genuinely loving relationship. Don't let overthinking and fear affect all the wonderful things you have to look forward to in life."

Despite Nikki's sage advice, Eve left less confused about her decision to come out but with more issues to consider when that time came.

❖

Lynette gazed over at the clock beside her bed. It was almost two o'clock in the morning. She had to catch a flight in just a few hours for a workshop she was teaching for their Miami subsidiary office. If she didn't fall asleep soon, she'd be useless. She punched at her pillow, tossing and turning, trying to find a comfortable position, then sighed in frustration. She was wide awake and there was nothing she could do about it. She'd been fine until a beautiful face she hadn't seen in weeks invaded her sleep.

She had been dreaming of sitting at a table in a bookstore signing copies of a book. She'd just been handed a book and asked who she was signing it for. The woman said "Eve" and Lynette had gazed up to find Eve Monroe, naked and glistening with moisture as if she'd just stepped out of the shower, standing before her. Lynette had woken up to find herself so intensely aroused she knew if she just reached under the covers and touched herself, she would orgasm, so she just lay there waiting for the feeling to pass. Unfortunately, it wouldn't be so easy to stop the ache in her heart. Lynette wondered how she could have fallen so hard in such a short time. She'd been so careful to keep her heart under lock and key after Marisol to avoid making the same mistake again. Yet within just a couple of weeks after meeting Eve, she'd unlocked the door, threw away the key, and didn't think twice about what she was getting into. What was it with her attraction to unobtainable women? First, Toni back in high school, then Marisol, and now Eve.

Lynette thought it would be so different with Eve, who'd seemed so sure and confident in her decision to be in a relationship with her. Yet, within a matter of hours, it all changed. One minute, Lynette was trying to convince her sister that this time would be different, and the next Eve was telling her she wasn't ready for an out and open relationship and Lynette was breaking it off before it even had a chance to start. She wondered if she'd been too abrupt in her decision to completely cut Eve out of her life after their last conversation. She of all people knew how difficult it was coming out to your family. After all, her father still refused to talk to her about her lifestyle or who she was dating. In the five years she and Marisol were together, he always found an excuse not to be home whenever they visited her parents.

Now that she was able to think more objectively about it, Lynette realized she should've been more understanding. Unfortunately, her heart had gotten in the way of common sense. She'd also probably ruined any opportunity of at least being a supportive friend. They hadn't spoken in almost a month when Lynette got the first call. She'd recognized Eve's number and refused to answer. After a few more attempts and messages, she stopped calling. Michelle said it was probably for the best, but Lynette was regretting not calling Eve back. She decided that would be the first thing she did when she returned from Miami.

Lynette was able to get some rest during her flight and somehow managed to successfully get through the first day of workshops on just a few hours of sleep. She turned down dinner with her team, trudging tiredly to her hotel room with plans to order room service and go right to bed. The two-day workshop was being held at the Delano Beach Club in Miami. Lynette had been looking forward to the event. She had planned to stay over the weekend to enjoy South Beach, but now all she wanted to do was get through the next two days and go home as soon as possible.

"Lynette?"

Lynette was just stepping onto the elevator and turned at the sound of her name to meet Eve's surprised gaze.

"Eve?" she said in disbelief, stepping out of the elevator. "What are you doing here?"

"I'm visiting family. What are you doing here?"

Lynette walked toward her. "Business meetings. I can't believe this. Are you staying at the hotel?"

"Yes. I thought I'd check it out as a future event location."

So many thoughts ran through Lynette's mind, the main one being how Eve looked even better than she remembered. She looked trimmer without having sacrificed her voluptuous curves. Her thick, curly hair was a lighter shade of brown than Lynette remembered with almost blond highlights. She wore a sexy, ombre gold halter sundress that came just below her knees with a pair of strappy, gold, high-heeled sandals. There was something else that Lynette couldn't pinpoint, but she knew it was more than just Eve's changed physical appearance.

"How've you been?" Lynette asked.

"I've been good. How about you?"

Eve's smile was soft and beautiful, causing Lynette's heart to ache painfully. That's when she realized what was different. Eve looked content. Her eyes were brighter, her face was more relaxed, and her smile was easy and free. Lynette didn't know what happened to Eve since they'd last seen each other, but whatever it was had obviously been good for her.

"I've been cool. Busy with promoting *Venus's Garden* and the usual hectic work schedule while trying to finish my current novel in progress," she said, sounding more self-assured than she felt.

"I read your interview in *OUT* magazine. You did great."

Lynette smiled shyly. "Thanks."

They quietly stood gazing at each other, Eve looking as unsure as Lynette about what to do next.

"Well, I guess I'll let you go. I just wanted to say hi. It was good seeing you again, Lynette."

"Uh, yeah, you too."

Their gazes held for another moment before Eve turned to leave. Lynette's heart screamed at her to do something, anything, just don't let Eve walk out of her life again.

"Eve, wait."

Eve hesitated then slowly turned around. "Yes?"

"Do you have a few minutes to talk?"

"I've been trying to talk to you for a while."

"I know. I'm so sorry I didn't return your calls. I just needed some time to figure out how stupid I was."

Eve grinned. "Why don't we go sit in the lobby. I'm meeting someone and don't want to miss her."

"Oh, okay," Lynette said worriedly. Had Eve found someone else already?

"I don't think you were being stupid, Lynette," Eve said after they sat down. "Despite coming to terms with my truth, I wasn't ready to be out, so it wouldn't have been fair to ask you to go back into the closet with me."

Lynette shook her head. "I should've been more understanding. You were going through a tough time. Coming out isn't easy. Instead of trying to be a friend and support you I shut you out."

"Okay, so let's agree that we both reacted badly to the situation. I don't blame you for shutting me out after what you'd been through with Marisol. Honestly, if you hadn't, I probably wouldn't have done what I needed to do at the time."

"What was that?"

Eve told Lynette about contacting Identity House for counseling, going to one-on-one sessions with a therapist Nikki referred her to, as well as attending her first group session before her trip to Miami.

"Wow, you've been busy," Lynette said.

Eve chuckled. "Yeah, I guess I have. I'm going to talk to my family when I get back home."

"That's great. No wonder you look so happy."

"Do I? Juliana said the same thing."

"Juliana?"

"Yes, that's who I'm meeting. She's the one who suggested I stay here. She lives in Miami but is going to stay at the hotel with me for my last few days here."

"That's great. I'm sure the two of you will have a good time." Lynette tried to keep a smile on her face and hoped the rush of jealousy she felt at the thought of Eve with another woman couldn't be heard in her tone.

Eve smiled knowingly. "There you go, jumping to conclusions. Juliana is my cousin."

Lynette felt her face heat with embarrassment. "That's right, you did say you were visiting family."

"Lynette, we had something really special. I hope I haven't ruined any chance of renewing it, but if I have, can we at least be—"

Lynette gently grasped Eve's face, leaned toward her, and kissed her, effectively cutting off anything else Eve was about to say.

Moving away just enough to gaze into Eve's eyes, Lynette asked. "You hope we can at least be what?"

Eve looked dazed and confused. "Friends?"

Lynette leaned toward her again, brushing her lips softly across Eve's. "Are you sure that's what you want?" she whispered.

"I want…"

Lynette stopped her assault on Eve's lips and locked her gaze with Eve's. "What do you want, Eve?"

Eve grasped Lynette's hands and placed them over her

heart. "I want you, Lynette. I want to be your friend and your lover, openly and unashamedly, no matter what my family says."

Lynette felt as if her world had finally tipped back on its axis. "I want the same thing."

This time they both leaned in for another soft, gentle kiss.

"I leave you alone for one day and all you can think to do is make out with strange women in the hotel lobby?"

Eve and Lynette abruptly broke apart, looking up at who interrupted their reunion. A beautiful, tall, dark-haired woman looked at them with a disapproving glare.

"Well, what do you expect? You're the one who told me to try and find something to distract me until you finished at the spa," Eve said.

"Honey, if I would've known this was the only thing you could think of, I would've locked you in your room. Who is this hussy with her lips all over my cousin?" The woman gave Lynette an angry leer.

Eve chuckled as she stood and pulled Lynette up with her. "Juliana, this is Lynette. Lynette, this is my very protective cousin Juliana."

Juliana's eyes widened in surprise. "*The* Lynette?"

"Yes," Eve said.

Juliana boldly checked Lynette out and smiled. "You were right. She's a nice little package. I see why you fell so hard."

"Juliana!" Eve said. "You'll have to excuse my cousin. She's missing that little mental pause button that makes you stop and think before speaking."

Lynette chuckled. "Reminds me of my sister Michelle." She offered her hand to Juliana. "Nice to meet you."

Juliana placed her long, manicured fingers in Lynette's hand. "Honey, I've heard so much about you I feel like I know you already. Why don't you join us for dinner and tell me if fate or coincidence brought the two of you to Miami at the same time in the same hotel."

Lynette's plans to order room service and go to bed early were forgotten. Having Eve back in her life suddenly gave her a renewed sense of energy. She found that she couldn't get enough of touching or looking at her as they had dinner with Juliana, who Lynette simply adored. She didn't mince words, readily speaking her mind on any and every subject they discussed. Especially when it came to warning Lynette if she did anything to break Eve's heart, she'd be on the next plane to New York to kick her ass.

After dinner they went up to the suite Eve and Juliana were sharing so that Juliana could change before taking Eve out to explore South Beach's nightlife.

"I really like your cousin. She and my sister would get along great," Lynette said when Juliana left them alone.

"I'm glad. She was a big influence in helping me figure things out."

"Really? How?"

Eve told Lynette Juliana's story and their family's reaction to her decision. "If she could make it through all of that with her sister as her sole support system, I can tell my family my own truth. If they find it hard to accept, the world won't come to an end, and I'll find a way to make it work with or without their support. I'm hoping it will be with it, but I have to prepare myself for if it's not."

Lynette brushed her knuckles along Eve's cheek. "You've come a long way since we last talked."

Eve turned her head, placing a soft kiss on Lynette's hand. "I had a little help and a lot to lose."

"Well, you'll be hard-pressed to get rid of me now. I'm in for the long haul," Lynette told her with a grin.

"That's good to know because we may be in for a bumpy ride once this weekend is over."

Lynette decided to extend her weekend after all to spend it with Eve. To her chagrin, Juliana insisted on playing chaperone, as she said, "to keep them out of trouble." Before they left Miami, Juliana made Lynette promise to continue to put their physical relationship on hold until after Eve spoke with her family. She would need the emotional support Lynette could give her more than the physical satisfaction. Lynette knew Juliana was right, but it didn't make it any easier, especially when a simple kiss with Eve could set her aflame. But she knew that Eve couldn't completely give herself to Lynette with the worry of her family's reaction hanging over their heads.

Chapter Six

Eve was the last to arrive at her parents' home for their family dinner. Her mother tried to arrange them at least once a month because she complained that other than holidays, it was the only way she would be able to see her children all together. Her stomach was in knots, but she somehow managed to make it through pre-dinner chatter and the actual meal without running from the house in a panic. Every now and then she would look up to find her mother watching her curiously, and then she'd gaze over at Paige, who gave her a supportive grin that only seemed to annoy rather than soothe her already wired nerves.

As soon as Eve came home from Miami, she called Paige and told her what happened during her trip and what she'd planned to do. Paige offered her love and support, telling her she'd be right there to help her through it, but somehow that didn't make her feel as secure as she thought it would.

After dinner she, Paige, and her brothers usually played cards with their parents watching to keep the peace. As they all went into the den Eve decided that would be a good opportunity to make her announcement. Once they were all gathered around the card table, she took a deep, shaky breath.

"Everyone, I have to tell you something."

"Keep it short, my luck has been running good lately and

I have a feeling I'm going home with a little extra cash in my pocket after this game," her brother Alex said.

Her brother Chris chuckled. "Sounds like Alex's new girlfriend has given him some newfound confidence."

Alex grinned. "You're just mad that she liked me better than you."

"Please, she's not my type anyway. You're the one that likes them all prim and proper. I prefer my women with a little flavor, like Paige over there," Chris said with a wink at Paige.

Paige laughed. "Honey, this is far more flavor than you could ever handle."

Tony playfully slapped Chris upside his head. "How are you gonna flirt with my wife while I'm sitting right here."

"Hey, I'm just letting her know that if she ever gets tired of your old ass, she can always come to me."

As soon as the words were out of his mouth Chris was out of his chair with Tony right on his tail. Alex instigated by cheering Tony on and Miguel just shook his head and kept dealing the cards.

"Enough, you two!" Eve's father's deep voice rose above the din. "You can wait until your sister finishes talking to kill each other. Until then, sit down."

Eve had been watching the playful banter with a smile, almost relieved to have the distraction, but her father's reprimand quickly brought everyone's full attention back to her.

"Go 'head, baby," he said with an encouraging smile.

"Thank you, Daddy." She nervously cleared her throat.

"I know you all have been worried about me since Stefan and I divorced. I just want you to know that I appreciate all the love and support you've been giving me in that time. I hope that after this conversation it'll continue."

"Uh-oh, this sounds serious," Chris said, getting a less playful slap in the head from Tony.

"I met somebody a little over a month ago. I didn't want to tell you guys until I was sure where the relationship was going. Well, it's getting pretty serious, and I wanted to make sure I talked to you guys before I introduced you."

"We've known you've been seeing someone for weeks. Tony told us," Alex said.

It was Tony's turn to get slapped in the head, but by his wife.

"What? I didn't know it was supposed to be a big secret," he said, rubbing his head.

"So, when do we meet this mystery man?" her father asked.

Here it goes, Eve thought to herself. "The mystery man is actually a woman."

A heavy silence settled over the room. The only ones who didn't have a look of surprise on their faces were Paige, who already knew, and her brother Miguel, which she didn't expect.

"Since it looks like no one else is going to ask, I might as well. Is this just an experimental thing or are you saying you're gay?" Chris said.

"Damn, Chris, do you ever *not* say the first thing that comes to mind?" Alex asked.

Eve looked in her parents' direction. She could see disappointment and hurt in her mother's tear-filled eyes and, surprisingly, understanding in her father's.

"I'm saying I'm attracted to women and currently dating one," she answered, not feeling the need to put a label on her attraction.

Eve watched helplessly as her mother stood and headed for the door.

"Mommy, wait," she called, but her mother ignored her as she hurried from the room.

Her father stood as well but walked over to her instead of following her mother and took Eve's face in his hands.

"Baby are you sure this is what you want?" he asked.

"Yes."

"Are you happy?"

Eve gave him a small smile. "For the first time in my adult life I can honestly say I am."

He nodded. "Then that's all that matters."

"You're not disappointed?"

"Yes, but I'll get over it. I love you, you're still my daughter, and who you choose to love won't change that. I've seen too many people, including your mother's family, lose their children because they couldn't accept the truth. I'm not going to be one of those. Just be careful and give me some time to talk to your mother," he said, placing a kiss on her forehead, then leaving the room.

"Boy, you sure know how to break up a party," Chris said.

"Shut up, Chris," Tony said.

"What about you guys?" she asked. "What are you thinking?"

"You knew I had your back from day one." Paige stood to give her a hug.

"You knew about this and didn't tell me?" Tony asked Paige angrily.

"I asked her not to, Tony. I wanted to make sure I was in the right frame of mind before I told any of you."

"You do remember what happened to Julian after he told the family he was gay?" Tony asked.

"Yes. Absolutely nothing. It was after she decided to transition that everyone treated her as if she had the plague.

I'm still the same Eve I've always been. I'm not going butch or transitioning to a man. I'm just not dating them."

Tony shook his head. "You're selfish, you know that? Mom and Dad have given you everything you could possibly ask for, and this is how you repay them?"

"Tony!" Paige exclaimed.

"How is accepting myself for who I truly am being selfish? I haven't done anything but be honest, with myself and them, and to be happy with whatever life I choose to live, which is how they raised us."

"They didn't raise you to be a dyke," he said angrily.

"Whoa, man, you're out of line now," Alex said.

Tony looked at Alex as if he'd lost his mind. "Out of line? You're okay with this?"

Alex shrugged. "Honestly, I don't see what's wrong with it. We all knew Eve was unhappy in her marriage. Before she met Stefan, you could count on one hand how many guys she brought home for us to meet. Bro, being gay doesn't make you a criminal. If Eve is happy, who are we to tell her she's wrong."

"I agree," Chris said.

Eve looked over at Miguel, who hadn't said a word. He was just a year older than her and the brother she was closest too.

"Miguel, you've been pretty quiet. What do you have to say?"

He shrugged and smiled. "I guess I've known since we were in high school, so I'm not surprised."

Eve looked at him in confusion. "What are you talking about?"

"Remember the summer we went on that camping trip to the Poconos with the youth group at the Y?"

Eve remembered that trip vividly, but she didn't see how that would've given Miguel any reason to be aware of her attraction for women. Unless…

"You knew?" she asked him.

Miguel nodded.

"Knew what?" Chris asked. "You can't bring up the possibility of a juicy story in front of us and not share."

Eve and Miguel both ignored their youngest brother.

"How? We made sure that we were as discreet as possible."

"Well, you were until the last few days of the trip. I overheard a couple of girls from your cabin talking about how you and Denise were sneaking out at night to meet some boys from another cabin. Daddy made me promise to keep an eye on you while we were there, so I stayed up to see what you were up to. I followed you guys to the rec room and saw you two together."

"Why didn't you ever say anything?"

"At first I was too shocked, and then I just thought you would tell us in your own time."

Tony stood. "I don't want to hear anymore. Mom left the room crying and you all are talking about this like there's nothing wrong. Eve, you're a grown woman. Live your life the way you want, but don't expect me to support it. I'll see you guys at the job site tomorrow. Paige, are you coming?" he asked angrily as he left the room.

Paige gave Eve an apologetic smile. "Let me talk to him. I'll call you tomorrow," she said, giving Eve a quick hug before following Tony out.

"He'll come around," Miguel reassured her.

"And if he doesn't, we'll beat him till he does," Chris said with a grin.

Although Tony's reaction hurt her, Eve was more concerned about her mother. Her father told her to give her mother some time before she tried talking to her. She took his advice and headed home, relieved that she'd finally been able to talk to her family but worried that she might have lost her mother in the process.

When she arrived home, Eve called Lynette to tell her how the evening had gone.

"How are you feeling?" Lynette asked.

"Relieved and sad. I know how conservative Tony can be, so I wasn't that surprised by his reaction, but for my mother to not even talk to me is hitting me harder than I expected."

"You want me to come over?"

"No, I think I just need to figure out my next approach with my mother."

"Okay. I'm here if you need me."

"I know."

After her call with Lynette, Eve noticed she had a missed call and a message that must have come through while she had been on the subway on the way to her parents' house.

"Hola, mija, I was just calling to see where you were. You're usually the first one here, so I just wanted to see if you were still coming. I guess you're on your way, so I'll see you when you get here. Te amo."

Hearing her mother's cheerful voice and loving endearment at the end of her message then remembering her silence and the disappointment in her eyes was too much for Eve. The enormity of what could happen as a result of what she'd told her family came down on her like a ton of bricks. She felt a tightness in her chest and a burning in her eyes that she tried fighting but failed miserably. First the tears, then the breathless pants of anxiety came as Eve realized that she could have possibly lost her mother in the same way Juliana had lost hers.

Although Cecelia's most adverse reaction was to Juliana's

transition, she still hadn't taken her coming out well. She'd thrown her out of the house and told her she was a shame to the family. They were still speaking at the time as long as they didn't discuss Juliana's other life. It wasn't until she started taking the steps to her transition that Cecilia had refused to speak to or see her.

Eve and her mother had always been close. She couldn't imagine not having that love and support whenever she needed one of those mother-daughter talks they shared so often. She didn't even want to think about the possibility that her mother would be so ashamed of her lifestyle that she wouldn't want to have anything to do with her. Eve didn't regret coming out to her family, but she did regret the possible loss as a result of doing so.

Overwhelmed with sadness, Eve sat crying for almost an hour. Even after the tears dried up, she found she couldn't move. When her intercom buzzed, she ignored the first and second notification. When it continued, she slowly pushed herself up off the floor, trudged over to the door and, without even bothering to ask who it was, buzzed her visitor up. She figured it was probably Paige anyway. A few minutes later, there was a knock at her door.

"Eve, it's Lynette."

"Lynette?" Eve opened the door and the relief she felt at seeing Lynette standing there brought the tears back to her eyes.

Smiling, Lynette held up a brown paper bag. "I know you said you didn't need me to come over, but I thought you could use some Häagen-Dazs chocolate chocolate chip ice cream and a strong shoulder to cry on."

Eve stepped aside to let her in. "I'm glad you didn't listen."

As soon as she walked through the door, Lynette opened her arms to Eve. "Looks like you need the shoulder more than the ice cream right now."

Eve walked into Lynette's embrace and felt as if the troubles outside her apartment couldn't touch her. This was what she wanted, needed, in her life. This was worth the risk of possibly shutting out those she loved. To be able to love someone fully without the fear she'd had before she'd decided to be honest with her family.

"How'd you know?"

Lynette kissed Eve's temple. "I could hear it in your voice."

Eve shifted within Lynette's embrace to gaze up at her. "How is it possible that you know me so well?"

"Because I know my heart, and you've become the reason it beats so strongly."

The intensity in Lynette's gaze and the smile on her face told Eve everything she needed to know. Lynette was in love with her. Eve felt the same. There was no need to put it into words, especially at that moment when Eve was going through so many other emotions, but it lightened her heart to know that although she'd fallen hard, Lynette was there to catch her.

Lynette placed a soft kiss on Eve's lips, then pulled away. Their eyes held for a moment before Eve kissed her this time. A need to be held, loved, and comforted came over Eve as her kiss grew more desperate, more insistent for a deeper response than what Lynette was giving her.

❖

Lynette responded, dropping the bag of ice cream on the floor, pressing their bodies so close to one another that she could almost hear Eve's heart calling out to hers. As if to say, *"Make me forget, even just for a moment, that nothing else matters but right here, right now,"* and needing so much to have this contact with another person.

The intensity of their desire was overwhelming. The promise Lynette made to Juliana to give Eve time was about to fly right out the window. Feeling Eve's warm, soft hands ease up her back beneath her T-shirt was almost Lynette's undoing. Somehow, she managed to tear her lips from Eve's, gently separating them. Seeing Eve's tear-streaked face had Lynette wanting to pull her back into her arms.

"Is there something wrong?" Eve asked.

Lynette wiped away a tear falling from Eve's beautiful brown eyes with the pad of her thumb. "No. I just think we need to slow it down a bit. We moved so fast in the beginning that I want to make sure that we're both truly in the right frame of mind before we take that next step."

Eve looked as if she would disagree then sighed. "I guess you're right. Will you grant me a favor, then?"

"I can try. What is it?"

"Stay and hold me for little while? I promise to keep my hands to myself," Eve said petulantly.

Lynette smiled. "I think I can handle that."

She picked up the bag she'd dropped and, following Eve to the kitchen, put the melting ice cream in the freezer. They walked arm and arm into the bedroom, took off their shoes, and lay on the bed. Eve turned her back toward Lynette, who gently pulled her against her own body. Their curves fit easily together, like the final two pieces of a puzzle. Lynette loved the feel of Eve's body against hers, and as much as she craved a more intimate embrace, this moment meant so much more. It showed that Eve trusted her not only with her body but also her heart.

❖

A few days went by before Eve's mother reached out to her asking if she could come by her apartment to talk. Eve rescheduled the few meetings she had for the day and tried to prepare herself for the worst. Her mother sounded so distant on the phone, however, the fact that she wanted to talk in person was a good sign.

"You painted since the last time I was here," Eve's mother said when she arrived.

"Do you like it?"

"It's very nice, brightens up the room."

"Would you like something to drink?"

"No, I'm fine."

They sat on the sofa with Eve's mother fidgeting with the placement of the back cushions.

Eve placed her hand over her mother's. "Mommy, please just talk to me."

Her mother nodded with a tired sigh. "I knew when you came by the day after your date that you were trying to find the nerve to tell me something. When you didn't say anything, I figured it couldn't have been important or you would've talked to me. The worst thing I could think of was that you were dating someone of another race. I could've never imagined that it was a woman."

Her mother looked so sad that Eve was almost tempted to stop her from continuing, but she knew they needed to have this conversation in order to move on.

"You know, it's funny, I always considered myself a very liberal woman until the moment you made your announcement. Suddenly, decades of strict Catholic upbringing took over and I could no longer see you as this strong, independent woman, but as my little girl who I'd somehow failed. Why else would she be willing to live such a life? At first, I wondered what I did wrong. Was there something I could've seen while you were growing up?" Her mother's voice caught, then she seemed to take a moment to pull herself together.

"Then I thought of my sister Cecelia. When Julian first told her he was gay, she called me hysterical. She wondered why God was punishing her with first taking her husband then making her only son gay. Was not having a father in his life the reason for it or was there something she did as his mother that made him that way? I told her that Julian being gay had nothing to do with any of that. It was just the way he was. It didn't make him any less her son. She wouldn't hear any of it. Told me that I'd spent too much time in America to know how wrong it was. Even when he decided to have the sex change, and I saw how hurt he was by his mother's reaction, I still believed that there was nothing wrong with his decision. It had been obvious to everyone but Cecelia that Julian wasn't going to be the son she expected him to be."

Eve's mother had been avoiding her gaze while she spoke, but she looked up now. "Then you made your announcement and I suddenly found myself looking through my sister's eyes. But unlike Julian, there were no signs. Even now I look at you and I wonder if it's true. There was nothing tomboy about you growing up. I couldn't even get you in a pair of pants if I tried. You were always my little girl and I thought we were always so close, yet, I didn't really know you at all. Why didn't you ever tell me what you were going through?"

"I couldn't even admit it to myself, let alone talk to you about it. Then when we went to Elena's wedding and Juliana showed up, I saw all your reactions. Even you were appalled by the changes she'd gone through. When Aunt Cecelia started screaming at her to leave and the only person who came to her defense was Elena…I was afraid that if I told you how I was feeling at that time, the confusion I was going through, we might end up like them."

"That was different, Eve. Julian—"

"Mom, she goes by Juliana now," Eve gently reminded her.

Her mother nodded and continued. "Juliana had left Puerto Rico as a man and came home as a woman. We were all shocked. I'm sure if we had seen her going through the process, we would've adjusted to it, but it was just such a surprise."

"It wasn't just that one incident, Mommy. Before Juliana's transition you all left her out of every family event. When I asked about it, I was shushed and told we don't talk about her or that I'll understand when I'm older. When I was old enough, I understood all right. I understood that being gay was not acceptable in this family."

"That's not true. It was easier on Cecelia if we didn't talk about her. It would send her into all kinds of rants."

It still bothered Eve that her mother continued to make excuses for her aunt's blatant disregard of her own child's feelings. "When was the last time anyone other than Elena has spoken to Juliana? Has anyone spoken to her since her transition?"

Eve's mother couldn't answer. The guilt in her eyes said it all.

"So, what makes you think it would've been any easier for me to tell you what I was going through? I met somebody and I suddenly saw how happy I could be, but knowing the price was possibly losing my family frightened me more than my own happiness. When that fear almost cost me Lynette, I had to decide what was best. Living a lie to make all of you happy or living the life that makes me happy. The decision wasn't easy, but with some counseling and reaching out to Juliana, I did what was best for me."

Eve's mother gazed at her curiously. "You spoke to him…I mean her?"

"Yes, she lives in Miami and is a very successful entrepreneur."

"Is she happy?"

"She says she is, but there's sadness in her eyes sometimes. She misses the family. Before I reached out to her, her only contact was with Elena."

Her mother looked guiltily down at her lap, nervously fidgeting with her fingers. "We were only trying to do what was best for Cecelia. We thought she'd eventually come around."

"But she hasn't. It's been almost twenty years and she's had no contact with Juliana whatsoever. Do you see why I was so afraid to tell you what I was going through?"

Her mother nodded. "Does Stefan know?"

"Yes. It was the reason we divorced."

Her mother gazed up at her with a look of regret. "I just wished you would've talked to me. We could've avoided all the misunderstandings."

Eve took her mother's hands. "I'm talking to you now."

"Are you sure about this?"

"Yes, surer than I've been about anything in my life. I'm happy, Mommy. For the first time in years, I'm content with who I am."

Eve's mother sat quietly for a moment. "This isn't going to be easy for me, Eve. I won't shut you out like Cecelia did Juliana, but I'm not going to be able to accept it as readily as your father has. My dream for you was to have the life I have, marry a good man like your father, have children who are as wonderful as you and your brothers, and live a happy life. It breaks my heart to know that I'll never see that happen.

I'm going to need some time, Eve," her mother said, the tears finally falling.

"I understand." She did understand but it didn't make it hurt any less. She was relieved that she hadn't lost her mother, but she also knew that their relationship might never be the same.

CHAPTER SEVEN

Eve was filled with nervous excitement. She and Lynette were spending a weekend in Key West. They'd decided that this trip, away from everyone, would be the weekend their relationship would move to a more intimate level. The previous relationships Eve had with women had been behind closed doors, so it was a new and exciting experience to finally be in an open one.

Since she and Lynette reunited, they'd focused on being an out and open couple, just enjoying being together, and getting to know each other on an emotional level. In that time, Eve had met Lynette's family, except for her father. He supposedly had something to do that was far more important than going to one daughter's house for an introduction dinner to meet his other daughter's girlfriend.

Lynette had also been introduced to Eve's family during her father's birthday dinner a couple of weeks ago. Eve's brother Tony had been cordial, but she knew from Paige that he was still having a hard time dealing with his little sister being in a romantic relationship with a woman. Eve's mother was also trying to accept her new lifestyle. To Eve's relief, her mother and Lynette hit it off quite well.

Eve took a deep breath, allowing the anticipation of the

evening to wash over her like a warm rain shower. They'd just returned from a romantic candlelit dinner at a small intimate restaurant and a moonlit walk on the beach near the resort. Lynette was in the other room opening a bottle of Eve's favorite sparkling wine and waiting for room service to deliver the chocolate-dipped strawberries she'd ordered. Lynette told her she wanted this night to be special for Eve and she was doing everything possible to make sure it was. After one last gaze in the mirror, Eve stepped out of the bathroom into their suite's bedroom.

❖

Lynette was walking in with a tray of strawberries when the sight of Eve halted her midstride. She wore a full-length, chocolate satin nightgown with lace trim along the very low-cut neckline that gave Lynette a mouthwatering view of lush breasts. When Eve moved toward Lynette, her shapely legs peeked from the gown's thigh-high slits and the satin material shifted seductively over her curves. Eve's skin appeared to be a richer, smoother caramel complexion than usual, which could've been as a result of the afternoon she'd spent lying by the pool. Whatever the reason, it had Lynette eagerly wanting to strip off the gown, lay Eve naked on the bed, and taste every inch of her.

Eve took the tray of strawberries from her. "Those look delicious."

"So do you." Lynette thought that she'd much rather have Eve than the strawberries.

With a teasing smile, Eve held the tray in one hand, picking up a strawberry with the other. "Why don't you have one of these," she held it up to Lynette's lips, "I'm sure they're much sweeter than what you're craving right now."

Lynette took a bite of the chocolate-covered fruit, her gaze locking with Eve's as she did. "Mmm...it's good, but what I want has more flavor and is much more satisfying to my appetite."

She put her arm around Eve's waist, leaned toward her, kissing her slowly, and then pulled away. "Now, that's more to my liking."

The tip of Eve's tongue slid over her lips. "You keep kissing me like that, I won't be able to keep my promise to let you set the pace for the evening," Eve said breathlessly.

Lynette chuckled. "Is that a promise?"

"Guess you'll have to kiss me again to find out."

Lynette gazed at Eve as if she seriously considered the suggestion, then smiled mischievously. "We've waited this long, I don't see why we can't wait until you at least have a glass of wine."

Lynette placed a light kiss on Eve's nose, took her hand, and led her toward the bed where a wine bucket stood. She took the tray from Eve, set it on the nightstand next to two champagne glasses, and then poured them each a glass of the chilled sparkling wine. Lynette held her glass up to Eve in a toast.

"To Eve, the woman who haunts my dreams nightly, fills my thoughts daily, and holds my heart always."

Eve looked dazed for a moment, then her face darkened with a blush. "Thank you."

Lynette allowed her to take a few sips of wine before taking the glass from her and setting it on the nightstand. She took Eve's hands, brought them toward her lips, and kissed each knuckle tenderly.

Lynette gazed into Eve's eyes. "This is your night, Eve. Let me love you as you deserve, worship you for the beautiful woman you are."

❖

Eve could only nod in response, words seeming to fail her under the intensity of Lynette's gaze. Her eyes and poetic words were doing far more to strum the strings of passion wound tightly within Eve than she ever thought possible.

Lynette's hands ran up the length of Eve's arms to slide the lacy straps of her gown off her shoulders. As the satin material fell in a pool around Eve's feet, Lynette's long fingers gathered in the hair at the nape of her neck, pulling Eve toward her. She covered Eve's face in soft kisses, her lips leaving heated imprints on her forehead, temple, eyelids, and cheeks before doing a slow perusal of her lips then traveling along her jawline to her neck, where she gently nipped and licked until Eve moaned softly.

Lynette stepped back, keeping Eve within arm's reach as her gaze sensuously perused Eve's body. Lynette's fingertips followed the same path her eyes had taken, down Eve's shoulders, to her aching breasts, along her waistline, over her hips, and ending where her gaze hadn't gone, over Eve's behind and up her back. It was a long, soft caress, but it was enough to send shudders of passion through Eve's body, making her legs too weak to hold her up. She grabbed on to Lynette's shoulders to steady herself, realizing that while she stood completely nude, Lynette was still fully clothed. Eve wanted to look at her the way she was being looked at. Touch her the way she was being touched. Make Lynette feel the same passion that ran along every vein in her body. With shaky hands, Eve slowly began to unbutton Lynette's shirt but found that her fingers refused to cooperate. Lynette grasped her hands, lowered her head to kiss her knuckles, and guided Eve to the edge of the bed.

"This is your night, remember? Sit back and relax, I'll do this."

Eve nodded, climbed onto the bed, knelt in the center of it, and watched as Lynette undressed for her. Lynette ran, biked, and played basketball regularly so she had a strong, athletic build, but it didn't take away from her feminine curves. Her breasts were half the size of Eve's but firm with large pebble-hard nipples. Her waist was narrow, curving out at her softly rounded hips; firm, tight buttocks; long, muscular legs; and, to Eve's surprise, completely waxed area at the juncture of her thighs. Eve thought Lynette was the sexiest woman she'd ever seen.

Seeing Lynette in all her naked beauty was Eve's undoing. When Lynette joined her in the bed, Eve pulled her toward her for a passionate kiss. Lynette coaxed Eve onto her back, laid the length of her body atop Eve's, and lowered her head toward Eve's breasts to take one of her nipples in her mouth. Eve moaned passionately as Lynette's warm mouth and flickering tongue sent flames of desire shooting from her nipples throughout her entire body. Lynette's intimate kisses traveled lower, down Eve's belly, stopping to nip and tease at her navel, and continued descending lower. The combination of her warm breath tickling the downy hair at the juncture of her thighs caused Eve's breath to catch in her throat, then release in a shaky sigh.

Lynette grasped Eve's hips, lifting them slightly off the bed, and made passionate love to her with the most intimate of kisses. It didn't take long for the first wave of pleasure to crash through Eve, followed by a second one so strong she grasped the bedspread for support as her body quaked from the intensity of her orgasm. As tiny aftershocks of pleasure continued to ripple through Eve, she reached down to nudge Lynette up from between her thighs, pulling her up to lie alongside her.

She kissed Lynette, tasting herself on Lynette's lips. It was more of an aphrodisiac than the strawberries, renewing Eve's arousal and bringing out a newfound aggressiveness.

❖

Eve gave Lynette a sexy grin. "I seem to find myself on the receiving end of pleasure quite often. Now it's your turn."

Lynette was just as turned on by giving Eve pleasure as Eve looked after having received it. "Mmm…I like the sound of that."

Eve reached over toward the nightstand to pick up one of the strawberries. After taking a small bite, she lowered the fruit to Lynette's breasts, spreading the sticky juice and melting chocolate over her hardened nipples, down the length of her abdomen, to finally dip playfully between the lips of her vagina. Lynette sucked in a breath, squirming beneath Eve's teasing fingers. She watched as Eve removed the strawberry, brought it to her lips, gazed directly into Lynette's eyes, and ate the rest of the fruit in one bite. It was the sexiest thing Lynette could have imagined anyone doing.

"Mmm…tastes much better with your sweetness," Eve said.

Without waiting for a reply, Eve slowly retraced the path she'd made with the berry, her tongue and lips leaving a heated trail of their own along the way. When she reached the now throbbing heat between Lynette's thighs, Eve lowered herself between her legs, kissing, licking, and sucking with a slow, easy passion, as if savoring every taste and flavor of an exotic dish. Lynette usually liked it a little harder, a little faster, but Eve was showing her that she was very capable of enjoying slow and easy. Her orgasm came on her like a slow burning fire that started where the tip of Eve's tongue teased, spread throughout her body, exploding from the core of her womanhood into a firestorm of pleasure-pain so intense she cried out Eve's name in ecstasy. As Lynette's body still trembled with pleasure, Eve slid her body up along Lynette's, who rolled Eve onto her back, slid her hand between their bodies, inserted one long finger into Eve's slick opening and her thumb over Eve's clit, and rode her until they both cried out hoarsely from their shared pleasure. Lynette gently withdrew her fingers, wrapped her arms around Eve's waist, and eased them onto their sides, keeping Eve within the circle of her arms.

Eve snuggled close and their legs naturally tangled together, as if needing to have every inch of their flesh in contact with the other. The openness and passion with which Eve had just given herself made Lynette's heart swell with emotion. Before tonight, Eve had given her heart; now she had gifted Lynette with her body. Both gifts, Lynette promised herself, she would not take for granted.

❖

Eve lay beside Lynette watching her sleep. They'd been dating for almost six months, and she still couldn't believe how happy she was. They had grown so much closer since their weekend in Key West. The last little protective guards that had been up were now gone and she willingly gave herself to Lynette mind, heart, and body. Neither had said the words that would seal the bond they had. There didn't seem to be a need to. It was as if Lynette knew what she thought or felt without her ever having to say it. They still spent hours talking or having friendly debates when they disagreed. They were also perfectly content just being together. Eve could be at her desk working while Lynette sat just a few feet away on the sofa working on her next novel. To Eve, it felt as if it was enough for them to know that the other was nearby if needed.

The physical part of their relationship was just as good. Lynette was a very attentive lover. So much so that Eve was beginning to think she was becoming addicted. Lynette's weekdays started early and sometimes went late, so they tried to spend weekends together, alternating whose apartment they would stay at. Eve tried her best to make up for the days they couldn't see each other, and whether it was a make-out session or full-blown lovemaking, she could never get enough of Lynette. So far Lynette had no complaints, but Eve realized she was going to have to slow down soon. She didn't want their lovemaking to become a chore, although the way Lynette had worked her last night with the vibrator Paige had given her had Eve thinking Lynette was just as addicted as she was. She was still a little sore, but it didn't stop the satisfied grin at the thought of it.

"What are you grinning like the Cheshire Cat for?" Lynette asked with a sleepy yawn.

"Just thinking that Paige had no idea how that vibrator would really be used when she bought it for me."

Lynette chuckled. "I still can't believe you had it sitting in the bottom of your closet for over a year. If I hadn't been fixing that shelf it would still be collecting dust."

"Well, I'm sure we managed to shake it off last night."

Lynette rolled onto her side, giving Eve a mischievous grin. "Wanna shake off some more?"

Eve smiled. "As tempting as that sounds, I have to meet your sister. We've slept most of the morning away and there's still quite a bit to do before your *surprise* party."

Lynette looked unconvincingly shocked. "Is that today?"

Eve swatted her arm. "Cute. If your travel schedule weren't so crazy, we wouldn't have had to tell you about it."

"What time is my mother conveniently bringing me home to make my grand entrance?"

"Seven."

"I still can't believe you talked me into allowing her to do a mother-daughter spa day."

"You'll enjoy it." Eve cuddled close to Lynette. "Besides, just think how touchably soft your skin will be by the time all your treatments are finished. I won't be able to keep my hands off you."

Lynette pulled Eve into her arms, burying her face in her neck. "Well, in that case, bring on the seaweed wrap and salt scrub," she whispered in Eve's ear before running the tip of her tongue along its outer curves.

Eve moaned as ripples of pleasure ran like electric currents through her body. "You keep this up, I'm going to be late."

Lynette's lips and tongue trailed down Eve's neck toward her chest. She took one hardened nipple into her mouth, sucking slowly, until Eve was shuddering with desire.

After releasing the nipple, Lynette made her way back up to Eve's ear, gently nipping her lobe, and then whispering. "Guess you better go shower, then."

Eve gazed at her as if she'd lost her mind, then playfully shoved her away. "You're gonna get it tonight."

Lynette raised an eyebrow. "Is that a promise?"

Laughing, Eve picked up her pillow, swatted Lynette with it, and scrambled out of the bed heading for the bathroom before Lynette could retaliate.

❖

Lynette watched the sway of Eve's bare bottom until it was lost behind the closed bathroom door. She was suddenly reminded of their date in the Hamptons when they'd showered and changed at her friend's condo. Smiling, Lynette climbed from beneath the covers, walked over to the bathroom door, and listened, just as she did that day. Only this time, after hearing Eve's lyrical humming, she didn't hesitate to turn the doorknob.

Eve had recently had her bathroom redone, installing a larger spa shower with clear glass doors that gave Lynette an unhindered view of her luscious curves. Eve turned, as if sensing Lynette watching her. Their gazes met, then were separated by a puff of steam. Eve watched Lynette walk toward the shower and open the door and stepped aside to give Lynette room to step in. Lynette took the soap-filled body sponge from Eve's hand and slowly washed her, sensuously running the sponge over her curves, front and back. Once Lynette was finished, she set the sponge aside and moved Eve under the spray of water. She proceeded to rinse the soap from Eve's body with just her hands, lingering for a moment along the curves of her breasts, nipples, and the soft hair at the juncture of her thighs.

Eve trembled with desire as she picked up the sponge, poured more of her liquid soap onto it, and gave Lynette the same intimate treatment she'd just received with one exception. Once Eve had rinsed the soap from Lynette's body, she eased her back against the shower wall, knelt before her, spread her legs, and brought Lynette to such an intense orgasm with her tongue and fingers that she grabbed onto the towel rack for support as her body rocked with pleasure.

Afterward, Eve stood, placed a soft kiss on Lynette's lips, and whispered against her ear, "Guess I better get dressed," before she walked out, leaving Lynette weak and trembling in the shower.

❖

Eve was still thinking about their shower when she arrived at Michelle's house.

"You're bright-eyed and bushy-tailed this morning," Michelle said.

Eve couldn't tame the smile she'd had all morning. "Guess I have spring fever."

Michelle snorted. "More like Lynette Fever."

"Still that obvious, huh?"

"Yeah, but don't worry, Lynette's just as transparent. It's nice to see you both so happy. To be honest, I had my doubts about you."

Michelle's admission surprised Eve. "Really? Why?"

Michelle shrugged. "I guess Lynette wasn't the only one who had to get over the Marisol breakup. I saw what it did to her, and I couldn't bear to watch her go through it again. Because you were still going through your own coming out issues, I didn't think you were what she needed at the time."

"What changed your mind?"

"Meeting your family during the holidays. Your mom is very observant. She could tell by the way I watched you and Lynette like a hawk that I had my doubts. She pulled me aside and told me why and how it was so hard for you to come out to them. Anybody willing to risk what you did to be with my sister isn't likely to turn around and say it was all a mistake."

"I'll have to thank my mother next time I see her. Lord knows that after what Lynette told me you did to Marisol, I don't want to be on your bad side."

Lynette grimaced. "She told you about that?"

"I guess she wanted me to understand why she was so stressed about you liking me."

Michelle pulled Eve into a half hug. "Well, you have nothing to worry about, especially since you don't have a car and my husband has forbidden me from ever buying spray paint again."

Eve laughed. She and Michelle spent the rest of the afternoon taking care of last-minute details for Lynette's party, including decorating her apartment while she was at the spa with her mother. As they were finishing up, Lynette's house phone rang. Eve couldn't ever remember hearing it ring the times she'd been at the apartment, so she forgot Lynette even had it, especially with her being such a technophile.

"It could be our mother. I told her to call the house phone since I tend to forget to charge my phone," Michelle said as she headed out to the living room to answer it.

Eve went about her task of folding napkins until she heard Michelle's quiet tone raise in anger. "You can't be serious!"

Eve walked back out to the other room just as Michelle slammed the phone back onto its charge stand. "Is everything all right?"

Michelle stared down at the phone as if she wished she could make it burst into flames with just a look. "I can't believe she'd have the nerve to call after all this time."

"I take it that wasn't your mother."

"No, it was Marisol. She said she was calling to wish Lynette a happy birthday and needed to speak with her. She's obviously lost her damn mind if she thinks I'm going to pass her message along to Lynette."

"It was a simple birthday wish. Nothing to get upset about." Eve hoped she sounded more confident than she felt.

Michelle gazed at her knowingly. "You don't actually believe that, do you?"

Eve shrugged. "No, but it's none of my business. If Lynette decides to return Marisol's call, I'll worry about it then. In the meantime, the caterer should be here any minute, as well as the guests, so we better finish up." She turned and walked back into the kitchen on shaky legs.

She tried telling herself that she had nothing to worry about, but her heart said otherwise. She hoped whatever Marisol needed to talk to Lynette about wouldn't come between what they've shared all these months.

❖

Eve was bent over, her stomach aching with laughter, as she watched her brother Chris and Lynette battle it out in the center of the living room as they did their best old school pop-locking routines. Chris had jokingly thrown down the challenge during a conversation about old school hip-hop versus new school and Lynette, after a few of her favorite imported beers, took him up on it. Eve and some of the other guests moved the furniture to clear enough space for the two of them to do their thing and were given quite a show for their efforts. The judge, a choreographer friend of Lynette's, was also laughing so hard she couldn't determine a winner, so a draw was called. Lynette walked over to where Eve sat and flopped on the floor beside her, laying her head on Eve's lap as she tried to catch her breath.

"Whew…I'm gettin' too old for this."

"Sit up so I can get you some water with a side of prune juice for your old bones."

Lynette swatted at Eve's behind as she stood. "Ha ha. Betcha this old lady can keep up with you."

Eve threw a sexy smile over her shoulder. "We'll see tonight when everyone's gone."

Lynette looked down at her watch. "Oh hell, in that case, let's start kicking them out now."

Shaking her head, Eve laughed and headed for the kitchen to grab Lynette a bottle of water. When she came back, Lynette was looking with a frown toward the front entryway. Eve looked in the same direction and saw Michelle in a heated conversation with someone at the front door.

Eve walked up to stand beside Lynette. "Who is it?"

There was a hesitation before Lynette answered, "Marisol," then walked toward the commotion.

Something cold and hard dropped in Eve's stomach. She set the bottle of water on a nearby table and quickly followed Lynette.

"I just want to see Lynette. I'm not here to crash her party," Marisol was saying but Michelle wouldn't hear any of it.

"If you don't leave right now, I'm gonna forget all my manners and smash this door in your face," Michelle said through gritted teeth.

"Michelle, what's going on?" Lynette asked.

"We have an uninvited guest that refuses to take my polite suggestion to leave."

"What are you doing here, Marisol?" Lynette asked.

Marisol gave Lynette a nervous smile. "I came to wish you a happy birthday and maybe talk."

Lynette rubbed her hands across her eyes with a tired sigh. "Now is not the right time. Besides, you've had several years to talk, and I haven't heard from you in all that time."

"I know, but a lot has changed."

Michelle gave a derisive snort. Lynette gazed at her in warning. Michelle gazed back at her as if she'd lost her mind.

"You've got to be kidding me. You're not actually falling for this shit," Michelle said.

"Why don't you go back to the party. I'll handle this," Lynette told her irritably.

Michelle shook her head then turned to leave. When her

gaze met Eve's, the look of anger in her eyes was replaced by pity. She placed a comforting hand on Eve's shoulder as she walked by. When Eve turned back around, Lynette was watching her.

"Can you give me a minute?" she asked with an apologetic smile.

"You sure?" Eve asked.

Lynette nodded. "I'll be right in."

Eve glanced back at Marisol, who looked at her curiously then turned away as Lynette stepped out into the hall with her.

"What was that all about?" Paige asked. "Lynette's sister walked by me looking like she was ready to strangle someone."

"Marisol is here. Lynette's out in the hall talking to her."

"Was she invited?" Paige said, wide-eyed.

Eve shook her head, glancing worriedly back at the door. "Did you meet her?"

"No, but I saw her."

"Are you okay?"

Eve tried to give her an encouraging smile. "I'm fine. I'll be right back."

Eve went to Lynette's bedroom. Closing the door, she leaned up against it and took a deep breath to clear the knot in her chest. Insecurities she'd never experienced before entered her thoughts. Despite how they broke up, Marisol and Lynette had a history. This was the woman Lynette had once planned to have a family with. In addition, Marisol's tall, softly curved figure—wide, hazel doe eyes; pert nose; full, pouty lips; long, rich, dark hair; and sun-kissed complexion—had to be far more tempting than her short height, thick figure, untamed hair, and average features. If Marisol was trying to come back into Lynette's life, how was she going to compete? Eve walked over and fell back onto the bed. She didn't know how long she was there, but a soft knock on the door brought her out of her self-imposed funk.

She sat up with a sigh. "Come in."

Lynette poked her head into the room. "Hey."

"Hey."

"You plan on coming back out to the party?" Lynette asked with a smile.

Eve could see the cheerfulness didn't reach her eyes. "I don't know. It was getting a bit crowded."

The smile slid from Lynette's face. "She's gone."

"Is she?" Eve's question wasn't as simple as it sounded.

Lynette walked into the room, shut the door behind her, and sat beside Eve. "She said she just wants to talk. I told her it would be best to come back tomorrow."

"How do you feel about that?" Eve asked.

"I don't feel anything about it," Lynette said unconvincingly.

Eve looked into Lynette's eyes. For the first time since they began dating, she found them unreadable.

"I see. Well…" Eve stood and headed for the door. "You've got a room full of guests, so we should go."

"Eve, wait."

"Yes?" Eve looked at Lynette expectantly but was met with silence.

Putting on her best hostess smile, Eve offered Lynette her hand. "We'll talk later."

Lynette looked as if she wanted to say something, then seemed to change her mind. Taking Eve's hand, she allowed her to lead her from the bedroom.

CHAPTER EIGHT

Later never came. By the time they finished cleaning up, Lynette and Eve were too tired to do anything but take their clothes off and fall asleep. Then, the following morning, Eve had a bridal shower brunch to coordinate, so she left before Lynette had completely woken up. She'd given her a kiss, told her she'd be back as soon as the event was over, then left. Lynette thought it was probably for the best. She wouldn't have been able to explain anything to Eve because she didn't understand what was going on herself. All she knew was that the moment she'd seen Marisol standing in the doorway of her apartment looking as good as she did the day that she'd walked out that same door had her pissed, confused, and her heart aching all at the same time.

It seemed obvious to pretty much everyone that Lynette was distracted after she and Eve returned from the bedroom, so the party broke up earlier than was planned. Lynette found it funny that as Paige and Eve's brothers, Chris, Alex, and Miguel, were leaving they gave her a curt good night and a warning look while Eve received comforting hugs and kisses. Even her own sister, who stayed to help with the cleanup, warned her not to screw things up with Eve. From their reactions she would've thought Lynette had personally invited

Marisol to the party. Lynette lay in the bed until late morning, then quickly showered and dressed. She couldn't help but think about what she and Eve were doing twenty-four hours earlier in Eve's shower. She knew mornings like that one would continue to be a memory if she allowed old feelings for Marisol to interfere with what she and Eve now shared.

When Marisol arrived later that afternoon, Lynette found it difficult to dispel the nervous flips in her stomach. She could see that Marisol was just as nervous. Good, she thought. Why should she be the only one suffering through this?

They walked into the living room with Marisol sitting on the sofa while Lynette tried to stay as far from her as possible by sitting in a chair on the other side of the coffee table.

"How'd your party go last night?" Marisol asked.

"Let's cut the polite small talk, Marisol, and just get to the reason why you've decided to show up on my doorstep after all this time."

Marisol looked taken aback but nodded. "Okay. I want to apologize for the way things ended between us. My family was pressuring me *to do the right thing*, threatening to cut me off. I felt as if I had no choice."

"You could've just been honest with me and told me all of this then."

"Lynette, you met my parents. You know how they are. They only put up with my lifestyle because they thought it was just a phase I was going through after what Gerron put me through while we were married. When my mother started having heart problems, my father blamed me. He said that I was breaking her heart living the way I was and not giving her the grandchildren that she deserved." Marisol lowered her head guiltily.

"I'm their only child. All I had to do was ask and they gave me anything I wanted, and I was going against everything they believed was right by having a relationship with a woman. They played the guilt card, Lynette. I was too afraid to call their bluff."

Marisol gazed at Lynette. Her bright hazel eyes sparkled with unshed tears, pulling at Lynette's heartstrings. Lynette shook her head, trying to rid the spell Marisol was still able to weave around her. When that didn't work, she stood up, turning her back on Marisol, and hopefully the feelings she was bringing up, to gaze unseeing out the window.

"Marisol, why are you telling me this now? I could've forgiven everything if you'd just talked to me back then. Instead, you had me believing you were ashamed of us, of what we shared. That you were doing exactly as your parents thought, using me to get through whatever your ex-husband did to you."

Lynette turned to find that Marisol had gotten up from the sofa and stood directly behind her. She didn't turn away this time. She allowed Marisol to see all the hurt and pain she'd caused in her eyes.

"I gave you everything, Marisol. Just like your parents, all you had to do was ask." Lynette's voice broke and tears she'd promised she'd never shed for this woman and what she'd done slid down her cheeks. "I loved you more than I ever loved anyone, and you made me feel ashamed of it. Had me doubting myself and what I'd wanted for as long as I could remember. Now you come back here thinking an apology and the real reason you left is going to make up for all you put me through?"

Marisol reached up to gently wipe a tear from Lynette's face, her hand lingering on her cheek. "No, I don't think it will make up for what I did, but I hope it's the first step." Her hand slid slowly from Lynette's face to grasp her hand.

"I also came to tell you that I told my parents I refuse to

live the way they want me to. I'll love whoever I want to love and couldn't care less about their money or what they think is right or wrong."

Lynette gazed at Marisol in confusion. "What do you mean?"

Marisol smiled affectionately up at Lynette. "I told them that I never stopped loving you and that I made a mistake leaving the way I did. I know it's probably too late and you've more than likely moved on, but is there any chance of us getting back together?"

Lynette's eyes widened in disbelief. "You're serious?"

Marisol's smiled broadened. "Yes." She grasped Lynette's hands. "We can be together now. We can do all the things we talked about doing, getting married, having a family."

Lynette couldn't believe this was happening. "What about the man you were having the affair with?"

Marisol's smile wavered. "There was no one else. That was my mother's idea. She hoped that if you thought I went back to sleeping with men, it would deter you from trying to get me back."

Lynette shook her head. "This can't be happening."

"It could if you let it. I never stopped loving you, Lynette. No matter how hard I tried, I could never get you out of my heart. If we could just start over, work our way back to what we had before my parents' interference, I'll prove to you how serious I am about sharing my life with you. I'll shout it to the world if I have to," Marisol said, wrapping her arms around Lynette's waist and laying her head against her chest.

Lynette's body seemed to have a mind of its own. Her arms came up around Marisol's petite body. Her chin rested atop her head just the way it used to when they held each other. The protectiveness she'd always felt for Marisol from the moment they met, the way Marisol shifted to look up into

Lynette's eyes in that *take me, I'm yours* gaze she was so good at, wheedled its way into Lynette's doubts.

"I'm here, Lynette, for as long as you want me, I'm here."

Lynette took a deep, shuddering breath. She could fight words, she could even fight physical attraction, but could she fight the memories of how good they'd been together before everything went so wrong? For a just a moment, Lynette thought of what could've been if Marisol had only been honest with her, but the lies and hurt were just too much to overcome, especially now that she knew what a true and honest love felt like. She gently grasped Marisol's shoulders and pushed her away.

"No, I won't do this to myself or Eve."

Marisol looked at her in confusion. "Who's Eve?"

"Eve is the woman I love and that I'm not about to betray. You need to leave."

"Leave? What about us and everything I just told you?"

"There is no *us*, Marisol. There stopped being an *us* when you walked out that door and left me with nothing but lies and a broken heart. Nothing you just told me changes any of that," Lynette said angrily.

Marisol shook her head. "I know you don't believe that. I could see it in your eyes. You still love me."

Lynette sighed in frustration. She needed to get Marisol out of here before things got ugly. "It's true, I still care about you, but we can never go back to what we had, Marisol, besides me being with Eve now, there's too much hurt and time between us to even try."

"Fuck Eve!" Marisol said viciously. "Do you realize what I sacrificed to be with you?"

Lynette looked at Marisol as if she didn't know her. "I didn't ask you to do that. That was your decision. We haven't spoken to or seen each other in years. Then, because you finally decide that being honest with yourself is more important than Daddy's money, you walk in here expecting us to just pick up where we left off. Real life doesn't work that way, Marisol. You aren't always going to get what you want with just a snap of your pretty little fingers."

"How could you be so cruel?" The tears gathered once again in Marisol's eyes.

"Marisol, I'm not trying to be cruel, just honest. Something I wish you had been years ago."

"You're making a big mistake." Marisol angrily wiped away the tears, smearing her eye makeup in the process. She looked down at the smudges on her fingers, grabbed her purse to search through it for something, then turned back to Lynette.

"Can I use your bathroom?" she asked, sniffling pitifully.

Lynette was hesitant to let Marisol stay any longer than necessary, but she looked like a sad raccoon and she felt sorry for her. "I'm sure you remember where it is."

Lynette watched Marisol walk back to the hallway that led to the other rooms in her apartment—her bedroom, home office, and bathroom—then turned back toward the window. As she watched the traffic moving along on the street below, she thought about the day she'd met Marisol.

❖

Due to train delays, Lynette was running late for a meeting and rushed off the subway taking the stairs up two at a time. To her annoyance, pedestrian traffic was at a standstill when she reached the escalators due to a family of tourists who obviously didn't know the main rule of escalating. The right side was for standing, the left was for walking. The family of four and their bags took up an entire three rows of stairs, casually chatting and holding up foot traffic. Lynette pulled out her phone and texted her manager when someone else's phone dropped next to her foot on the stair.

"Oh my God, I'm so sorry. Would you mind grabbing that for me?"

Lynette looked down at the phone then up at the most beautiful eyes she thought she'd ever seen.

"Uh, yeah." She knelt, picked up the phone, and handed it to the woman.

"Thank you so much. This is crazy. My first day at a new job and I'm going to be late. I've been trying to call my new manager, but she's in a meeting." The woman looked as if she were about to cry.

"I'm sure she'll understand. I'm running late also. Since my manager used to live here before she moved to Jersey, she's completely understanding. I'm sure yours will be also."

"I hope so because I still have to find my way there when I get out of here. I haven't commuted for work in years, so I'm a little out of practice."

"If you don't mind me asking, where are you headed? Maybe I can direct you once we get up top." Lynette had no idea if this woman was gay, but she was gorgeous, and a casual chat to find out wouldn't hurt. If anything, she would be doing her good deed for the day assisting the woman.

"Ten Columbus Circle."

"Really? That's where I'm headed. What company?"

The woman narrowed her gaze at Lynette, as if wondering if she should trust her.

"I work at Wolf Technologies on the twenty-second floor," Lynette said to reassure her she wasn't trying to stalk her.

The woman's eyes widened in surprise. "Me too!"

"Great, we can walk over together."

Chatting as they walked, Lynette learned that Marisol would be working in her department as an assistant to one of her fellow managers. She also found out Marisol was married when she got a glimpse of her ring finger as she checked in with building security. She was disappointed but figured it was probably for the best. She had a rule to keep her work and personal life separate, and getting involved with Marisol would've shot that all to hell, so they became good friends while Lynette continued crushing on her from afar.

❖

Lynette wished she would've held to the separate work and personal life rule the day Marisol came to her place to make dinner. That was the start of what Lynette had hoped would be something beautiful and lasting but turned out to be a heartbreak she didn't realize she still felt the remnants of until now. Her relationship with Eve was becoming everything she had wanted with Marisol, yet Lynette still wondered what might have been. Up until their final year together, despite Marisol not being fully out, their life together was good. Lynette had even learned to overlook the moments Marisol could be clueless or downright blind to other people's feelings. Lynette had written it off to the fact that she was an only child and was spoiled by her wealthy and indulgent parents because she was rarely that way with her. Love truly was blind, Lynette thought. She turned from the window and looked back toward the hallway wondering what was taking Marisol so long.

"Marisol, are you alright?" Lynette asked as she walked toward the hall.

Lynette's office was the first room on the left and the bathroom was across from it on the right. She stared into the empty room in confusion. Lynette looked down the hall and noticed her bedroom door at the end of the hall was partially closed, which wasn't how she'd left it. With long strides, she quickly covered the distance from the bathroom to her bedroom.

"Marisol, I don't have time for games," Lynette said in annoyance as she pushed the door opened and was stunned to find Marisol sitting naked on her bed. "What the hell are you doing?"

Marisol's eye makeup had been cleaned up and reapplied. Her lips looked as if they had received a fresh coating of lipstick as they curved up into a sexy smile. She stood and sauntered confidently to Lynette.

"I thought you might need a little reminder of how good things were between us." She lifted the bottom of Lynette's T-shirt with one hand and slid the other under it and up her abdomen.

Lynette grabbed her wrists to stop her. "No, get dressed and get out," she said in barely controlled anger.

Marisol had the nerve to look confused. "You want me to leave?"

"Yes. Did you really think you could pull this stunt off after what I just told you?"

Tears gathered in Marisol's eyes again. Lynette didn't know how she never noticed how quickly Marisol was able to bring on the crocodile tears.

"Please, Lynette, don't do this. I can't—" Marisol shook her head, covered her mouth with her hand, and whimpered.

"You can't what?" Lynette didn't even know why she was standing here talking instead of getting Marisol out of the apartment.

She wasn't worried about Eve coming back for another couple of hours, but the more she let this fiasco continue, the more unnecessary drama she was adding to her life.

Instead of answering, Marisol threw herself at Lynette, wrapped her arms around her waist in a vise-like embrace, and planted her lips on Lynette's. It was so unexpected that Lynette was slow to react. It was only a moment, but it was a moment that she would forever regret when she heard the apartment door open.

❖

Eve walked into the apartment surprised not to find Lynette vegging out in front of the TV watching her murder mystery shows as was her Sunday afternoon ritual if she and Eve didn't have plans to go out.

"Lynette?" Eve called out. "She must be working in her office," she said to herself, heading toward the hallway, which was steps from the front entryway.

"I know I said I'd call first but—" Eve had just turned the corner where she heard a fiercely whispered, "Shit!" and was met with the sight of Lynette pulling another woman's arms from around her.

"I guess I should've called," was all she could think to say as she realized the other woman was Marisol, naked.

"Eve—"

Eve held up her hand. "Don't." She turned and felt like she couldn't get out of the apartment fast enough as she fumbled with lock.

She managed to get the door open just as Lynette ran out after her.

"Eve, wait. Let me explain."

Eve continued walking down the hall to the elevator, her eyes burning with tears she refused to cry. At least for now. She wanted to leave with as much dignity as she could muster without committing murder or at least an assault.

"Please, Lynette, not now. I don't think I could bear to hear any explanations right now."

She pushed the button on the elevator, then looked around for the stairwell. Before she could reach the door Lynette grabbed her arm.

"It's not what you think."

Yanking her arm from Lynette's grasp, she turned on her so fast her head spun. "It's not? So, I didn't just walk in on you and your completely naked ex-girlfriend looking guilty as hell? That's not her lipstick smeared across your mouth?"

Lynette attempted to wipe the lipstick away instead of immediately responding to Eve's questions.

That was too long in Eve's opinion. "Yeah, that's what I thought," she said quietly, then continued to the stairwell.

Lynette's apartment was on the eighth floor, which gave Eve the time she needed to tamp down the pain and anger she felt rising so that she could make it home without breaking down. She hailed a cab, knowing she couldn't handle a long subway ride uptown, and barely kept it together. She kept seeing Marisol's perfect naked body and Lynette's guilt-ridden face, and her imagination added scenarios she tried not to let gain traction in her head. Had they just finished making love or were they just starting? Was it sudden or planned?

Eve recalled the look Michelle had given her when Marisol had come by the apartment last night. Had she been a fool to believe Lynette when she said she was over Marisol? Should she have stayed to hear Lynette out? *Yeah, while Marisol was getting dressed. I don't think so.* What could Lynette possibly say to explain what she'd walked in on that would make Eve believe it wasn't what she'd seen? She covered her mouth to hold back the scream that was rising up in her throat and could practically hear her heart cracking and breaking in her chest.

❖

Lynette could only watch as the woman she loved disappeared through the stairwell door and possibly from her life. Her feet felt as if they were filled with lead as she trudged back to her apartment. All she wanted to do was curl up in bed and pray this was all just a bad dream. Unfortunately, seeing Marisol finally dressed and standing in the middle of her living room was like a slap of reality.

"You need to leave, Marisol."

"Lynette—"

"Marisol, the way I'm feeling at this moment, if you don't walk out that door right now, I will not be responsible for what I say or do next," Lynette warned her.

Marisol picked up her purse. "I'll call you later when you've had time to calm down."

"Don't bother. I told you there was no going back, and I meant it. Getting involved with you brings me nothing but heartache."

Their gazes held for a moment. Then, with a sigh, Marisol shook her head and left. As the door closed behind her, Lynette finally had the closure she needed on their relationship, but at what cost?

When Eve had left Lynette's apartment, she couldn't bear to go home. She also couldn't bear the thought of talking to Paige or her mother about what happened. Paige was so protective she'd probably want to confront Lynette. Eve's mother had just recently begun asking how she and Lynette were doing, something she never did before, so neither could be objective about the situation. Without a second thought, she called Nikki from Identity House from the cab. A few minutes later, Eve was heading to Nikki's apartment instead of home.

She managed to hold back the tears for the entire ride but broke down on Nikki's doorstep.

It took some time before Eve was able to get any words past the lump in her throat as she sobbed in Nikki's arms. When she did, Nikki listened with her usual attentiveness then took a moment before speaking once Eve was finished.

"I know you're hurting and it's difficult to imagine what reasonable explanation Lynette could give for what happened, but I think you should give her the opportunity to do so. It could be easy to just walk away to lick your wounds, but if you do, then you're only cheating yourself of the closure you need to end things if that's what you intend to do."

Eve sniffled and wiped her already raw nose. "I know you're right and it makes sense, but just the thought of seeing her again feels like someone is twisting a knife in my heart."

"That's understandable. You're probably going to continue feeling like that until you do see her and find out what's going on. From what you've told me about Lynette, she really didn't have closure from her relationship with Marisol. That their breakup was as sudden and surprising as what you're going through. Maybe, as wrong as it may seem to you, this was Lynette's way of getting closure."

Eve snorted in derision. "You're telling me she had to cheat on me by sleeping with the woman who cheated on her and broke her heart in order to get closure?"

Nikki gave her a sad smile. "Like I said, it may not seem right to you, but you won't know what was going through Lynette's mind at the time until you talk to her. Also, I thought you said you caught them standing in the doorway, with Lynette still fully dressed and Marisol naked."

"Does it matter where I caught them? They could've just been finishing, or I walked in and stopped it before it happened. Either way, they were in each other's arms standing in the doorway of Lynette's bedroom. It couldn't be more obvious what happened," Eve said angrily.

"On the surface, that could be true, but there could be more to it than that. There's only one way to find out."

What Nikki said made sense, but the pain of heartbreak was too intense to let reason seep in, so Eve left Nikki's with no more relief than when she arrived. Now, hours later, she lay curled up in bed wondering how it was possible to have any more tears left after an afternoon of crying. She thought her tears had more than dried up until she lay in bed and Lynette's scent drifted up from the pillow she'd slept on the other night. It wasn't the racking sobs she'd gone through earlier, but a slow, steady flow brought on by the sadness of loss. Lynette had become such an integral part of Eve's life that she couldn't imagine what it would be like without her.

CHAPTER NINE

Lynette called her several times over the next few days. Eve let the calls go to voice mail. She knew Nikki was right about giving Lynette a chance to explain, but in a matter of days, Eve went from grieving her lost relationship to anger over what Lynette had done. She just didn't want to hear any excuses that would only lead to the same conclusion: Lynette had betrayed their love and Eve's trust.

Lynette wasn't the only person Eve blew off. When Paige or her mother called for their frequent chats, she claimed she was too busy and would call later. Even Lynette's sister, Michelle, who Lynette had confided in what happened, called to see how she was doing. Eve told her she didn't feel right talking to her about the situation. Michelle told her she understood and to give her a call if she changed her mind. Eve focused on the one thing she could count on, work. Work didn't let her down, betray her, or break her heart. Focusing on other people's joyous celebrations made her forget, just for a little while, how unhappy she'd become.

Then Juliana called and with one simple question, "How are you and that sexy girl of yours doing?" it reopened the wound Eve had unsuccessfully tried to bandage by not acknowledging it. She tearfully told Juliana what happened, and a few days later Juliana was standing in her apartment, suitcase in hand.

"Juliana, you didn't have to fly up here. I told you I'd be fine."

She waved dismissively. "Honey, I didn't just do this for you. I've never been to New York, and this was as good an excuse as any to visit."

That made Eve smile for the first time in weeks. "All I have to offer is my sofa bed."

"I've slept on worse. Now, tell me how we're going to handle this Lynette situation."

"*We're* not going to do anything. Lynette made her choice the minute she decided to sleep with Marisol."

"You haven't spoken to her yet?"

"No. I don't think I can listen to whatever excuse she'll come up with."

"If you haven't spoken to her, then how do you know she even slept with the hussy?"

"I know what I saw, Juliana."

"I didn't ask you what you saw, I asked what you knew."

Eve sighed in frustration. "First Nikki, now you. Why the insistence that I give her a chance to explain anything?"

"Because when we're in love and hurting, our minds tend to play tricks on us and we may only see half the truth of what's really going on," Juliana said sagely.

Eve quirked a brow. "What happened to you kicking her ass if she did anything to hurt me?"

Juliana shrugged. "That was before I saw how much in love you two were. I honestly don't think Lynette would do anything to purposely hurt you. I think you need to look at the situation and take into consideration that even though she's obviously a hussy, this Marisol woman represented a part of her past that she never had the chance to bring closure to."

"Is that what you flew all the way up here for? If it is, you just wasted your money."

Juliana smiled. "You are definitely a Rivera, just as stubborn as the rest of us."

Other than Paige and Lynette, Eve had no other female friends, so it was nice having Juliana there. Sometime the following night, Eve woke up to a loud crash from the other room. She jumped out of bed and raced to the living room.

"Juliana, what's going on? Are you all right?" It was dark, so all she saw was Juliana's long shadow in the apartment's entryway.

"I'm fine but I don't know how long whoever I have lying on the floor will be," Juliana said breathlessly. "Get the lights and call security."

Eve hit the light switch, ran over to the intercom system, and gazed down to where Juliana was straddling someone's back with their arm twisted up behind them.

"Security," a voice said on the other end of the intercom.

"Sorry, Frank, false alarm."

"No problem. Oh, and Miss Folsom is on her way up. I think she had a bit much too much to drink."

"Thanks," Eve said, then hung up. "It's Lynette," she told Juliana.

Juliana looked at her in confusion, then down at the person beneath her.

"Hey, Juliana." Her speech was slurred.

"Hey, Lynette. May I ask what you are doing sneaking into my cousin's apartment in the middle of the night?"

Lynette twisted her head slightly, looking up at Juliana with glazed eyes. "Are you gonna let me up?"

"Not until you answer my question."

Lynette laid her head back on the floor. "She won't return my calls, so I thought I'd pay her a visit."

"And you couldn't have done that at a respectable hour? You had to not only ruin my beauty sleep but also my fifty-dollar manicure?"

"Will an apology and a check for fifty bucks make up for it?" Lynette asked.

"Maybe after you take a shower and drink a few cups of coffee to sober up. I could smell the alcohol on you as soon as you walked in," Juliana said as she released Lynette.

Eve watched as Lynette was slow to get up and wobbly once she did make it to her feet. The drunken glaze seemed to clear for just a moment as she looked at Eve.

"God, you look good. I miss you so much," Lynette said, slowly walking toward her.

"You're drunk." Eve put her hands up to stop Lynette from coming closer.

"I know. It was the only way I could get up enough nerve to come here."

"I wouldn't talk to you when you were sober, what makes you think I'm going to talk to you now?"

Lynette looked confused for a moment.

Eve sighed tiredly. "Go home, Lynette. Have Frank get you a cab and go home."

"I can't. I love you too much to just walk out of here without at least trying to talk to you."

Eve closed her eyes to fight back the tears threatening to flow. For this to be the first time she heard those three words was too much.

"Were you thinking about how much you love me when you were with Marisol?" Eve asked angrily.

"Yes…I mean no…shit, this isn't coming out right at all." Lynette shook her head as if trying to clear the confusion that shown on her face. All that seemed to do was make her stumble. She caught herself on the arm of the sofa.

"Eve, you can't send her back out like this. She may not even make it home," Juliana said as she walked toward Lynette to help steady her.

"She got here with no problem, I'm sure she'll be fine," Eve said half-heartedly. She knew Juliana was right. She'd never seen Lynette this way before. Tipsy, yes, outright drunk, no.

Juliana must've seen Eve giving in. "I'll put her in a cold shower."

Eve nodded in agreement. "Some of her sweats and T-shirts are on the second shelf in the closet."

As Juliana practically carried Lynette toward the bathroom, she moaned loudly.

"I think I'm gonna be sick," Lynette said, covering her mouth and suddenly finding enough balance to run to the bathroom on her own.

Juliana wrinkled her nose at the retching sounds that followed. "I'll make sure she doesn't make too much of a mess."

"No, I'll do it," Eve said wearily. She felt somewhat responsible for Lynette's current state.

"You won't get any argument from me," Juliana said. "I'll go make some tea. Coffee might be a bit much once she's finished."

"Thank you." When Eve walked in, Lynette was sitting on the floor with her cheek resting against the bowl of the toilet.

"This isn't how I planned this at all," she said weakly.

Eve turned on the shower. "A lot of things don't go as we plan. We just have to accept them and move on." She turned and met Lynette's now perfectly clear gaze.

"Have you moved on, Eve?"

Eve looked away. "Can you manage the shower on your own or do you need me?"

"I need you, Eve, but not for the shower. I need you back in my life."

"Lynette, this is not a conversation to have while you're sitting here drunk, covered in your own bile, in the middle of my bathroom."

Lynette grabbed onto the sink to pull herself up. "I can handle it from here."

"I'm sure you remember where your extra clothes are," Eve said on her way out.

Once she closed the door, Eve leaned against the wall, covering her mouth to keep the sob she'd held back from escaping.

After her shower and some fresh clothes, Lynette felt more like herself as well as embarrassed at her behavior. Some of her friends had come by with a case of her favorite beer hoping to cheer her up. Lynette didn't know how many she drank. She'd stopped counting after the first six, but it had only made her more depressed. That's when she made the drunken decision to see Eve. One of her friends, afraid Lynette would end up in trouble trying to get there on her own, ended up driving her. She now realized it had been the wrong thing to do and she'd probably just given Eve even more reason not to take her back. She walked out into the living room to find Eve and Juliana sitting at the dining table.

"Have a seat. We saved a cup for you," Juliana said with a welcoming smile.

"No, I think I'm just gonna catch a cab and head home. I've caused you guys enough trouble for the night."

"You're probably not going to find many cabs this late,

you might as well stay. Juliana can sleep in the bedroom with me while you take the sofa bed," Eve offered.

Their gazes held for a moment.

"Besides, I think we should talk," Eve said.

Juliana stood. "That's my cue."

"Thanks, Juliana."

"For what? Almost breaking your arm?"

Lynette chuckled. "For not breaking it."

Juliana grinned. "That two years of self-defense training came in handy. Now you two play nice. I'm up way past my bedtime and I'm a bitch when I don't get my beauty sleep."

"Good night, Juliana," Eve said.

Juliana placed a motherly kiss on her forehead. "Good night, cuz. Take it easy on her. I think she's been through the wringer enough tonight."

They both watched Juliana leave, then gazed at each other. Eve looked as unsure as Lynette felt.

"Your tea is getting cold," Eve said.

Lynette sat in the chair across from Eve and took a few sips of her tea. She gave her a small smile. Honey and lemon, just the way she liked it. Even now, after what happened, Eve was still taking care of her.

"Thank you," she said.

"You're welcome."

They sat quietly sipping from their mugs for a moment then Eve set hers aside.

"So, what happened?" she asked Lynette.

Lynette told her everything. From the moment Marisol arrived until she'd made her leave. As she spoke, Lynette wondered what Eve could be thinking. Her face was so calm and unreadable.

"So, nothing happened between you two?"

"I swear, Eve, nothing happened. What she did was just as surprising to me as it was for you to walk in and see us that way."

Eve quirked a brow. "I doubt that, but I understand what you're saying. I'm going to ask you something and I need you to be honest with me, Lynette."

"Of course."

"Are you truly over Marisol? Is there any chance, after what she told you, that you would consider getting back together with her?"

Lynette took a moment to think about her answer. She wouldn't lie to Eve, but she also didn't want to hurt her more than she already had. "I thought I had gotten over her. Thought that there was nothing she could do or say that would make me understand how she could profess to love me one day and the next tell me it was all a lie. Then she told me what happened and why she lied. For a moment, I thought about what could have been if she'd only been honest with me from the beginning and whether I still had feelings for her. Then I thought about you and what we have now, and as much as I still care for Marisol, nothing she could do would make me give that up."

Lynette could see the doubt in Eve's eyes. She couldn't blame her. She could only imagine how she would've reacted if the situations were reversed.

"I believe you that nothing physical happened between you and Marisol, but I don't believe you've moved on as much as you think. For you to even consider, just for a moment, what it would be like to be with Marisol again proves that. I trusted you, Lynette. When Marisol showed up the night of your birthday party, I didn't say a word. When you asked me to give you a minute to talk to her out in the hall, I didn't say a word. Then, when you told me she would be coming back the next day, I wanted so much to tell you no, I won't allow that, but I had no right. I had to trust that you were over her and that if there was any chance that you weren't or that you wanted to go back to her, you would talk to me." Eve wiped a stray tear from her eye before it could fall.

"I did something that day I never did before. I left an event I organized in the hands of my assistant planner because all I wanted to do was get back to you. I had a feeling that the only reason Marisol would come back after what she'd done was to try to get you back, and I'd never told you how much I loved you." Eve chuckled bitterly. "As if the words would act like some charm to keep the evil away."

"I'm so sorry I hurt you, Eve. I'll do whatever it takes to make it right. Just tell me what you want," Lynette pleaded.

Eve looked so sad. "Can you turn back time and change what happened?"

"Eve…"

"I didn't think so."

They were at an impasse, and Lynette could feel what they had slipping through her fingers like sand, and she had no idea how to stop it. She reached across the table to grasp Eve's hands and found some relief in the fact she didn't pull away.

"I admit that I made the wrong decision in how I handled Marisol. I should've talked to you and been honest about what I was feeling when I saw her again, but I didn't know what I could say that wouldn't sound like I still loved her. Give me time to prove to you that she's gone for good. That I do love you and only want to be with you."

"Lynette, I don't know how to get past the fear of Marisol wanting you back. We've only been together for six months. You and Marisol have years between you. Years of a love deep enough to make you want to marry her and have a family. A love deep enough for her to turn her back on everything to be with you." Eve's hands slid from Lynette's grasp. "I truly do love you, but I don't know if I can compete with that. I can't bear to continue putting my heart on the line only to be hurt in the end."

Lynette closed her eyes, fighting back tears. She'd finally had the chance to say all the things she'd never gotten to when Marisol walked out of her life, and now that she was able to put her past to rest, her future was slipping away. Irony was a bitch.

Eve stood. "Maybe, with some time, I'll feel different, but right now…"

"I understand," Lynette said.

"You're still welcome to stay since it's so late."

Lynette's heart throbbed painfully. To stay with a literal and figurative wall between them was too much for Lynette to deal with now that she had sobered up. "Thanks."

As soon as Eve closed her bedroom door, Lynette picked up her clothes and left.

❖

As she heard Lynette leave the apartment, Eve felt as if her heart would threaten to stop beating at any moment. The tears she'd managed to mostly hold back while they were talking sprang free, blurring her vision, and soaking into her pillow. She curled up in a ball on her side of the bed, trying to cry quietly so she wouldn't disturb Juliana, but her pain and grief was too much to bear. It released with a shuddering sigh and loud whimper. She felt the bed shift shortly before Juliana wrapped an arm around her waist and stroked her hair soothingly.

"Let it all out," Juliana said.

"Why does it hurt so much?" Eve wailed.

"Honey, that's why they call it heartbreak."

Eve didn't think there was anything left to break, but she was obviously wrong as she cried herself to sleep.

The next morning, Eve awoke to the sound of Juliana singing along to the sultry voice of Calma Carmona and the aroma of coffee and other delicious scents that she found her stomach growling happily for because she had barely eaten since the Marisol incident. If it couldn't be eaten raw, she just skipped it because she didn't have the motivation to cook. Her diet had consisted of fruit, coffee, and protein bars to get her through the day. Her eyes felt like sandpaper from all the crying, and her pillow was crusted with mucus and tears. With a tired sigh, she threw her covers aside and plodded into the bathroom.

One look at her wild hair; red, baggy eyes; and crusty nose almost had Eve crying again, but she took a deep shaky breath, sucked up the misery, and took a hot shower. After, she combed the knots from her hair, tied it back into a bushy ponytail, threw on a pair of sweats and a T-shirt, and let her hunger lead her into the other room. She wasn't surprised to find that Lynette wasn't there. Eve heard her leave shortly after she'd gone to her room. She hoped Lynette had gotten home safely and wished the night could've ended with them kissing and making up, but Eve didn't know how that was possible under the circumstances.

"There she is. Just in time for a good old-fashioned Rivera breakfast. The cure-all for many a woe," Juliana said cheerfully. "I hope you're hungry."

Eve looked down at the platters Juliana was placing on the kitchen island and couldn't help but smile. The first was a platter of sliced mango, pineapple, and strawberries. The other was a family favorite prepared the morning after any major event such as birthdays, funerals, and weddings. The dish was called huevos revuelto con salchicha, scrambled eggs with sausage, but the Riveras had a tendency to throw in whatever else they had available, so Eve didn't ever remember having the same dish twice. Juliana was no different. She'd added shrimp, chorizo sausage, tomatoes, mushrooms, and peppers.

"Was all of this in my refrigerator?" Eve couldn't remember when she had last gone grocery shopping.

"Everything but the fruit and chorizo. I borrowed your keys and got that from the grocery store down the street."

"I'm impressed. First day in New York and you're already venturing out on your own."

Juliana shrugged. "I noticed the store when the car service passed it when I arrived. Now, café con leche or plain?" She held up the coffeepot.

Eve smiled. "Con leche, please."

"Smart choice."

Once they were seated and eating, Eve felt less like the emotional wreck she'd been.

"Are you ready to talk about it now?" Juliana asked.

"Nothing much to talk about." Eve told her Lynette's explanation of what happened.

"Well, now you know she didn't cheat, and it was all the hussy's fault trying to seduce her."

"Not all of it was Marisol. Lynette and I made a promise to be open and honest with each other from the beginning so that there were no misunderstandings and chances of hurting one another the way Marisol had hurt her. Lynette wasn't open about what she was feeling about Marisol when I asked her about it the night of her party, so I guess that promise only applied to me." Eve stabbed angrily at a piece of pineapple.

"Maybe she was confused and didn't know what she was feeling."

"That's fine. I would've understood that if she just talked to me, but she didn't, leaving us in the situation we're in now."

"So, what, after one major issue, you're done? If that's the case, my dear cousin, you're in for a lifetime of heartbreak because love and relationships aren't perfect. Those imperfections and how you cope with them will either strengthen a relationship or kill it." Juliana reached across the table and took Eve's hand. "I know you love Lynette, and it's pretty obvious she loves you, especially when she could've just as easily fallen for Marisol's scheming, but she didn't. She chose you. That should count for something."

Eve knew Juliana was right. She had pretty much done to Lynette what Lynette had done to her when she was trying to deal with her feelings for Lynette and the fear of coming out to her family. She'd assumed the worst about what happened with Marisol, walked away, then ghosted her without even giving her an opportunity to explain. Tears blurred her vision. She was so sick of crying.

"I was a selfish bitch, wasn't I?" Eve said.

Juliana gave her an understanding smile. "This is your first love. You were guarding your heart. No one would blame you for being a little selfish."

"I wouldn't blame her if she never wanted to see me again."

"You won't know that unless you talk to her."

Eve gave Juliana's hand a gentle squeeze. "Thank you again for being here."

"You don't have to thank me. It's what family does."

"Speaking of family, I told my mother you were in town."

Juliana slid her hand from Eve's. "I think we need to freshen up our coffee." She left the table to grab the coffee pot. There was a tremor in her hand as she refilled their cups.

"She wants to see you."

Juliana slowly sat down and looked nervously up at Eve. "She does?"

"Yes. We could go today if you like. I think I've put her off long enough about what's going on with me. If I don't go to her, she's going to show up here. If you're not ready for that, then I can go alone." Eve said.

Juliana pasted on an overly bright smile. "Well, I came here for excitement. What better way to kick it off than with tackling your girlfriend and family drama?"

Eve stood, walked over to Juliana, and wrapped her arms around her shoulders. "It'll be fine. We'll be fine."

Eve didn't know if she was trying to convince herself or Juliana, she just knew that it had to be okay. She loved Lynette too much not to fight for her, and she believed Juliana deserved a family that loved her no matter what.

❖

Lynette's phone buzzed as soon as she turned it on when her flight to London landed. Seeing Eve's name pop up on the screen for a missed call, voice mail, and text message brought all the heartache she was hoping to leave behind for the next month. She had been offered the assignment of leading a project to assist in building a manufacturing company's new international office in London and train their IT staff on the new system a month ago and had planned to fly Eve in for the last week of the assignment. Lynette was going to tell her the day after her birthday party, but everything fell apart.

She waited until she got to her short-term stay apartment to listen to and read Eve's messages because she didn't want to break down on the plane with nowhere to go until they reached the gate. She read the text message first.

Lynette, please call me. I'm sorry. I love you.

She read the message twice. Why was Eve apologizing to her? She was the one who screwed up. Eve didn't owe her any apologies. She listened to the voice mail next.

"Lynette, I'm sorry I didn't give you a chance to explain about Marisol before jumping to conclusions. I freaked out because I didn't think I could compete with what you two shared, so I ran to avoid being hurt. I selfishly didn't think of how that would hurt you. I'm so sorry. I hope you'll forgive me and that you would be willing to talk things over. I would completely understand if you don't after how I treated you last night. Please call me."

"Oh, Eve," Lynette said miserably.

She could hear the pain in Eve's voice and wished she could hop in a car and run over to Eve's apartment to hold her, tell her she loved her, and that she would do whatever it took to make things work with her. Unfortunately, it was kind of difficult to do that from across the Atlantic Ocean. Lynette looked down at the time on her phone. She originally wasn't supposed to leave New York for a couple of days after her drunken visit to see Eve, but after what happened she wanted to get as far from New York as possible and managed to change her flight to the following morning. It was currently eight o'clock at night London time, which meant it was three in the afternoon in New York.

Lynette's finger hovered over her phone, her heart beating a mile a minute. She took a deep breath and pressed *Call Back*.

Chapter Ten

Eve walked into Peaks, a high-rise restaurant at the Hudson Yards in Manhattan, excited about meeting her potential wedding client. When they had called her that morning asking to meet that afternoon to discuss potentially planning their daughter's wedding within the next month, she considered turning them down. Then they mentioned their $75,000 budget and already having the venue booked, and she decided it was worth the short notice. They chose to meet for lunch at Peaks because the wedding was going to be held in one of their event spaces. As she was being escorted to the table where her clients waited, her phone buzzed in her bag. She reached into her bag, then stopped. Whoever it was would have to wait until after her meeting. This would be the biggest wedding she had ever coordinated, and she wanted to be focused on the client. In the back of her mind, Eve worried that Lynette hadn't returned her call or text. Honestly, she wouldn't blame Lynette if she never wanted to speak to her again, which hurt but was her own fault.

Eve mentally shook herself out of the sadness setting in and put on her best smile as she neared a table where a well-dressed, distinguished-looking older couple sat. At her approach, the man, sporting a neatly trimmed mane of salt-

and-pepper gray hair and dressed in a well-tailored gray suit, stood and offered Eve his hand.

"Ms. Monroe, right on time. I'm a stickler for punctuality, so you've already gained a point," he said with a charming smile.

Eve shook his hand. "I'm glad to hear it. It's a pleasure to meet you, Mr. Vasquez."

"This is my wife, Lourdes," he said, indicating the woman sitting beside him.

Her hair was also salt-and-pepper and styled in a tight bun that lay at the nape of her neck in intricate twists. She wore a burgundy designer pantsuit that Eve had considered getting her mother for Christmas until she saw the price tag. Eve offered her hand.

"It's a pleasure to meet you, Mrs. Vasquez."

She smiled pleasantly and her perfect French manicured hand was soft and warm. "Likewise. Please, sit, and call us Thomas and Lourdes. Our daughter is running a little late and should be here any minute. In the meantime, do you have a portfolio of your work that you can show us? As I mentioned during our phone conversation, I've seen some of your work from the Conner Foundation Charity Ball I attended, which was very grand and elegant, but I would like to see what you do for weddings."

"Yes, of course."

Eve took her iPad out of her bag and pulled up the video portfolio of weddings she showed to clients. She updated it after each wedding to ensure she wasn't showing out-of-date events. When it came to weddings, something that was big last year could already be out of style this season. Wedding trends were as fickle as fashion trends.

"Mom, Dad, I'm so sorry I'm late," a breathy female voice interrupted.

Eve's back was to their new arrival, so she stood and turned to face who she hoped would be her next client and received the shock of her life.

"Not to worry, Marisol. Eve was just showing us some of her work," Mrs. Vasquez said. "Eve, this is our daughter Marisol, the bride-to-be."

Eve was relieved her back was to Marisol's parents so they wouldn't see her shocked expression before she managed to school it back into a pleasant smile. "It's a pleasure to meet you, Marisol, and congratulations on your engagement."

It seemed to take Marisol a little longer to recognize her, but Eve knew when it happened, and she enjoyed the moment Marisol's pleasant smile turned to nervousness.

"Uh…yes…it's a pleasure to meet you as well and thank you. It was sudden," Marisol stammered.

Mrs. Vasquez chuckled. "Sudden, please, this was the third time her fiancé, Randall Scott, proposed in the past year. The only thing sudden is the wedding date, which I still don't understand why you insist on having so soon. An outdoor summer wedding would be so much better."

Marisol slid her hand from Eve's grasp and shifted her gaze to her parents as she sat in the seat beside hers. With a calmness she'd developed working with irate patients at Stefan's office, Eve managed to keep smiling while all she could think of doing was smashing her fist in Marisol's beautiful face. She kept her professional demeanor as she sat back down and continued with her presentation. Afterward, Mr. Vasquez signaled the waiter over and they ordered lunch. Eve could see it was just as torturous for Marisol as it was for her as she spotted her practically shredding her napkin in her lap. They chatted about décor ideas, with Mrs. Vasquez doing most of the talking while trying to pull Marisol into the conversation to get her opinion.

"You know what I like, and you and Dad are paying for it so I'm sure whatever you choose will be fine," Marisol responded to her mother's recent attempt to include her. "If you'll excuse me. I need to make a trip to the ladies' room."

Eve watched what direction she went in and turned back to Marisol's parents. "If you'll excuse me, I think I'll do the same."

"Maybe you can get her to tell you want she wants," Marisol's mother said in annoyance.

Eve smiled. "I'll see what I can do."

Eve waited outside the stall area in a small lounge probably set up for ladies to sit and fix their makeup or chat before heading back out to dine. No one else seemed to be in the bathroom because Marisol was the only one to exit a few minutes later. She stopped suddenly in the doorway as she met Eve's glare.

"So, how did you expect everything to turn out if your plan worked?" Eve asked calmly, although her blood was boiling.

"That's none of your business." Marisol headed toward the main door.

Eve was closer and cut her off. "It is my business since you were so intent upon breaking up my relationship while you were engaged to someone else. Did you really tell your parents you wanted to be with Lynette or was your fiancé your backup plan in case your seduction didn't work?"

Marisol looked away guiltily. "You wouldn't understand. You've been with Lynette for what, like a few months? She and I have a history." She looked back up at Eve with a little more surety. "She still loves me. She just needed a little push to be reminded of that. If you hadn't walked in, I would've had her."

"And then what?" Eve asked, genuinely curious now about what Marisol had planned.

Marisol didn't answer.

"Let me take a guess at what your plan was. Get Lynette back, then somehow manage to convince her to continue to keep your relationship on the down low while you marry Randall to satisfy your parents and keep your fortune. How'd I do?"

Marisol's confidence seemed to wane at the possible truth being thrown back at her.

Eve shook her head in disgust. "You know what you are, Marisol? You're a user with no consideration of the people you claim to care for in order to get what you want. Lynette deserves better than that. Better than you."

Marisol snorted, looking haughtily down her nose at Eve. "You think you're better than me? I probably have more money in my purse than you do in your entire back account."

Eve shrugged. "You probably do, but do you know what you won't have and what money can't buy you? Lynette's love."

Marisol went from haughtiness to being on the verge of tears. Eve felt bad for the verbal slap, but it only lasted for a moment as she remembered why she was here and what Marisol had planned to do to Lynette.

"This isn't going to do anything but end badly. Judging by your mother's questions, I believe she's seriously considering hiring me. You need to come up with an excuse as to why you would like to continue interviewing other wedding planners because if she decides to hire me, I'm, regretfully, going to have to turn her down after I had already told her I was available before you arrived. I'm sure you wouldn't want me having to explain why. Now, I'm going to thank them for lunch and leave because I don't think I can continue this farce any longer." Eve walked out of the ladies' room without a backward glance.

When she returned to the table, she used the excuse of having another meeting that had been scheduled prior to the Vasquez's call that morning. It wasn't really a lie. She was meeting her mother and Juliana to look at properties. Juliana was considering opening a sister spa to her Miami location in New York, and Eve was looking for office space as her business was beginning to outgrow her corner desk in her apartment. Having the Vasquezes as a client would've been a big boost not only to Eve's client referral list but also toward how much office space she could afford. Despite that, she wasn't willing to sacrifice her soul by signing a deal with the she-devil that continuously played with Lynette's heart.

As soon as she stepped onto the elevator, Eve took her phone out of her bag and cursed out loud at the missed call. Lynette had finally called her back and she had let it go to voice mail. She listened to the voice mail with a frown.

"Hi, Eve. I got your voice mail and text. I'm sorry it took so long to respond, but I was on a flight to London when they came through, so I didn't get them until after I landed. I'll be here for the next month or so, and with the time difference I'm not sure when we'll be able to catch each other, but I would love to talk to you. I'll try to catch you tomorrow afternoon my time, which will be in the morning for you. I hope you're doing well. I..."

Eve waited with bated breath at Lynette's pause, trying not to anticipate the words that would follow.

"I'll talk to you tomorrow. Good night," Lynette said quickly before the click of her hanging up followed by silence tore at the scabs over Eve's heart.

❖

Eve took a car service downtown to meet her mother and Juliana at a retail space in Chelsea. They stood out front as she exited the car.

"There she is," her mother said, smiling happily.

"Sorry I'm late." Eve stepped into her mother's embrace and almost broke down.

"Juliana told me you had a last-minute meeting. Hey, are you okay?" her mother asked as they separated, and she spotted the tears Eve had tried to quickly blink away.

Eve managed a smile. "I'm fine, got a little something in my eye."

Eve's mother looked at her skeptically. "Mm-hm. We'll talk when we get back to the house." She looped her arm through Eve's as they walked to the door.

Juliana smirked as she held the door open for them. "Hey, girl."

Eve rolled her eyes. "Hey."

Eve knew she wouldn't get any sympathy there. She was thrilled to have been able to initiate reuniting her mother and Juliana, but because they had such similar personalities, she felt as if Juliana had become the older sister that she'd always wanted as well as her mother's co-conspirator when it came to advising on Eve's love life. Their reunion had been bittersweet. After the initial shock of seeing how Juliana had changed, Eve's mother had cried over how much Juliana looked like their grandmother when she was young. Eve had retreated to her father's home office to give them privacy. After an hour, Juliana had come to get Eve so that her mother could reprimand her for brushing her off since the drama with

Lynette happened. After Eve told her what happened, her mother had given her the same advice, almost to the letter, as Juliana. It had only been a day, but the two of them were already thick as thieves. Today had been the first whole day they'd spent together, and Juliana would be having Sunday dinner with the family before she headed back to Florida at the beginning of the following week.

After walking through the space with the Realtor, he took them to another retail space for Juliana and an office space for Eve in Soho. Afterward, they caught the subway back to Brooklyn, where they gathered in the kitchen for coffee and her mother's dulce de leche cheesecake.

"Now, tell me what's going on," Eve's mother said.

Eve sighed in resignation. She knew neither her mother nor Juliana would let it go if she didn't say anything. It must be a Rivera trait, she thought to herself. She told them about the meeting with Marisol and her parents and missing Lynette's phone call.

"You didn't call her back?" Eve's mother asked.

"No, Mommy. It's the middle of the night there."

"It was only around ten or eleven at the time you got the message," Juliana said.

Eve looked from one to the other. Both looked at her expectantly.

"Lynette said she had just landed. That was two hours after she called. I figured she was probably in bed already since she likes to arrive at international locations with time to get a full night's sleep before she works in the morning."

Juliana smirked. "I see. Auntie, Eve was just being thoughtful, not a chicken."

Eve couldn't help but smile. "Exactly. Besides, she said she would call me tomorrow morning, which gives me the whole night to figure out what I'm going to say to her that could possibly make up for how I treated her."

"I'm sorry and I love you usually works with your father," Eve's mother said with a wink.

Eve chuckled. "Thanks, Mommy, I'll remember that."

Her mother's teasing smile turned serious. She reached across the table and took Eve's hand. "I know it took a little time for me to accept you and Lynette being together, but I saw how happy you made each other, and I knew that you had finally found what your father and I have. Don't give up on it so quickly. If I had done that, your father and I wouldn't be together, and we wouldn't have had you and your brothers."

"What do you mean?" Eve asked.

Her mother gave her a hesitant smile. "When I first met your father, I did my best to deter him, despite my attraction. I tried to maintain a friendly distance, because I knew my mother wouldn't accept him being of another race. She had hoped I would return to Puerto Rico and marry a good, Catholic, fair-complexioned Puerto Rican man, to give her beautiful even fairer Puerto Rican grandchildren. But he was persistent." Her mother's smile broadened as she blushed down into her coffee cup.

"We dated for a year before I even mentioned to anyone in the family that I had a boyfriend. I sent a bunch of pictures home to my sisters, one of which was of your father and me after spending the day at the beach with some friends. I probably should've sent one taken before then because you know how much your father's complexion darkens during the summer after spending days out in the sun doing construction work."

Eve nodded. Her father's naturally sepia complexion darkened to a deep mocha every summer, and she still remembered the disapproving glances from her grandmother when they went to visit her mother's family for the summer. Eve and her brothers were never treated badly by their grandmother, but they never felt the love from her that they did from their grandparents on her father's side. Her father took it in stride, but Eve could see how much it bothered him that he had never been accepted by her.

Eve's mother continued. "The next time I went home, my mother threatened to never speak to me again if I continued to see your father. When your father insisted on meeting your grandmother, I put him off for as long as I could. We had been together for almost three years when, after dropping me off at the airport to go home for my mother's birthday, he showed up at the gate with a suitcase in hand. I had never told your father that my mother would not be happy with us being together. At that point I had already met his family and they were all so loving and welcoming that it made the thought of the animosity he would get from meeting my mother unbearable. I practically begged him not to board the flight with me. Told him it just wasn't the right time to meet my family. That all the focus would be on us instead of my mother's birthday."

Eve's mother's eyes sparkled with unshed tears. "We had our first major argument that day, and he accused me of not wanting to introduce him to my family because I was ashamed of him. I didn't know what to say because, in a way, I guess he was right, but not in the way he thought. I wasn't ashamed of him. I was ashamed of myself for not being able to stand up to my mother and proudly introduce the man I loved to my family. Your father left and I boarded the flight alone regretting having pushed him away. Maybe even for good. When I saw my mother, I told her that I loved your father and didn't care whether she approved of him or not. If she was willing to risk losing her daughter over it, then so be it. She barely spoke to me that entire trip, so I left a day early, anxious to get back home to your father. Unfortunately, he refused to return my calls or see me for weeks. If it hadn't been for your aunt Joan, I would've given up. She tricked your father into coming over to her place while I was there and pretty much forced your father to listen to me. I told him everything. About my mother's prejudice, that I wasn't ashamed of him, and that I loved him."

Eve's mother's tears had dried, and she grinned. "I even got down on one knee and proposed to him."

Eve couldn't believe it. "You didn't?"

Her mother nodded. "I did, but your father was too much of a gentleman to accept, but he had a surprise of his own. He had planned to propose to me after we returned from Puerto Rico and hopefully had gotten my mother's blessings. As we know, I screwed that up, but Joan was holding on to the ring for him, so he collected it and was down on one knee proposing to me."

Hearing that her mother had almost made the biggest mistake in her life by losing her father had Eve seeing her in a different light. "Why didn't you ever tell us this story?"

Her mother shrugged with an embarrassed look. "I guess I didn't want you all to see me as anything but your mother. Not some silly woman too afraid of her mother's disapproval to be with the man she loved."

"Because that would make you look human," Juliana said with a grin.

Eve's mother quirked a brow at Juliana. "Could also be a bit of pride." She looked back at Eve. "I told you all of that so that you don't make the same mistake with Lynette. Don't let pride get in the way of what could be a wonderful relationship.

There was so much left unsaid between your father and I that it almost put an end to our relationship. Be honest with Lynette and truly LISTEN to what she has to say."

Eve nodded. "I will."

"What about Marisol. Are you going to tell Lynette?" Juliana asked.

Eve didn't even need to think about her response to that. "No. Marisol has caused her enough heartbreak. I'm not going to help her add more to it."

Juliana looked pleased. "Good idea. Now, let's talk about how fabulous my new spa will be in that Chelsea location."

❖

Eve barely slept that night and woke up earlier than usual the next morning, anxious about her talk with Lynette. The extra half cup of coffee didn't help her already jittery nerves when her phone rang at eight a.m. and Lynette's name popped up on the screen.

"I believe that's my cue to hit the showers," Juliana said. They had been having breakfast together.

"Hi," Eve said.

"Hey," Lynette responded, then silence followed.

"How've you been?" they asked in unison.

Eve smiled. "I've been okay. How about you?"

"Same. We've been extremely busy here. Hit the ground running as soon as we walked through the door this morning. This is the first break I've had all day, but I didn't want to miss the chance to return your call."

"I appreciate that, but if you're too busy, we can talk over the weekend. I don't want to keep you from work."

"No, we're good. What did you...I'm sorry, can you hold on for a minute?"

Eve heard voices in the background. "Lynette, go. We can talk later."

"I'll try and call you when I get back to the hotel, if it's not too late."

"Okay. Talk to you then."

"Eve."

"Yes."

"It's really good to hear your voice."

It wasn't a lot, but it was enough to give Eve a spark of hope that Lynette still cared. "It's good to hear yours also."

They said good-bye and Eve sat at the table staring down at the time on her phone, willing it to speed up. As it felt like forever for a minute to tick by, Eve sighed in exasperation and went over to her desk to try to get some work done. She had three weddings, an engagement party, and a corporate retreat scheduled in the next couple of months that she needed to get work done for, as well as one last prospective office to visit in the same area of Chelsea as Juliana had chosen for her future spa location, so she had plenty of work to keep her busy. Despite all of that, her day still seemed to drag, but at least a couple of bright spots came out of it. Both she and Juliana signed leases for their rental spaces and would be working within just a few blocks of each other. They celebrated with dinner, then picked up a bottle of champagne for a toast on the rooftop deck of her building.

Eve huddled farther under the blanket she and Juliana shared to fight off the early spring chill in the air. "So, will you be commuting between New York City and Miami?"

Juliana grinned happily. "That's the plan for now. I'll go back to Miami on Monday, let my staff know the good news, then contact the contractor the Realtor recommended and schedule another trip up here to meet in person and go over plans. Once construction begins, I'll probably find a short-term stay apartment and split my time between the two until it's finished."

"Sounds like a great plan."

"Yeah. Hopefully, if my current manager of the Miami location is willing to take on the added responsibility, I'm going to leave the running of the spa in her hands and move permanently up here."

Eve looked at Juliana wide-eyed. "Really?"

Juliana's smile broadened. "Really. Being with you and reuniting with Auntie Pilar made me realize how much I miss having family around. Talking to my sister on a regular basis helps to ease the loneliness, especially when she comes for visits, but the moment she heads back home I'm alone again. I love my makeshift family in Florida, but there's nothing like real family to make a girl feel loved."

Eve grasped Juliana's hand under the blanket. "I'm so happy you'll be staying. Now I'll have two sisters, you and Paige."

"I'll never be able to thank you enough for reaching out to me. For connecting me with family again. First Elena, now you. You've both been my port in the storm of my crazy life."

Juliana snuggled closer to Eve and Eve wrapped an arm around her and laid her head on Juliana's shoulder.

"You can hang on to me whenever you feel yourself floundering. I'm here for you just like you've been here for me these past months. I don't know how I would've gotten through not only my coming out but what's been going on with Lynette without you. I love you."

"I love you too," Juliana said, her voice breaking with emotion.

CHAPTER ELEVEN

Lynette looked down at her watch for the third time in the past half hour. It was six o'clock at night London time and it seemed this meeting was not going to be wrapping up anytime soon. The contractors, architect, and her team couldn't seem to agree on where the server room should be located and how much space was needed. This was the second night in a row she probably wouldn't be getting back to the hotel until late. Too late to call Eve. It wasn't because it would be a late hour in New York when she called. It was that she would be too tired to have the conversation they needed to have. She wanted to be able to focus all her attention on Eve. Not be interrupted to handle an unnecessary crisis or too tired to stay awake during the conversation. Usually, Lynette was able to acclimate to a different time zone within a day of traveling to a location, but for some reason, she still felt jet-lagged when she woke up in the morning, which made the long days even more tiring. She knew it was probably the stress of the project as well as her and Eve's on-and-off relationship, both of which had been giving her fitful nights of sleep.

"Lynette, are you even listening?" Guy, the lead architect, said in frustration.

"I'm listening, but you obviously aren't. We told you

what we needed, Lance agrees," Lynette said, pointing to their contractor. "So, we just need you to get on the same page. I seriously doubt they need a fourth pantry. Just give us the added space so we can finish this job before the month is out and all get back to our lives."

Guy scowled at her. She was equally frustrated at the arrogant, chauvinistic Frenchman who, since she arrived, had been treating her as if she should be quietly sitting there looking pretty instead of leading a team of IT professionals on a major facility buildout.

Lynette pushed away from the table and stood. "I need a coffee."

She walked out of the conference room, took the stairs instead of the elevator from the tenth-floor offices, and headed out of the building. As she walked toward a Starbucks on the corner, she pulled out her phone and texted Eve.

I'm so sorry. I'm going to have to put off our call again. I really do want to talk to you, but I want it to be when I have time to sit down and focus on us and not work. This weekend, I promise.

She waited as the little conversation bubble started then disappeared and reappeared again with Eve's response.

Okay, I understand.

Lynette couldn't help but wonder what Eve was really going to say before the bubble disappeared the first time. She sighed tiredly and picked up her pace as the Starbucks attendant, who'd gotten used to her late night runs already, tapped his wrist to indicate they were closing soon. She really didn't need any coffee, but she'd needed an excuse to leave before she said something to Guy she probably wouldn't regret later.

Fortunately, they managed to come to an agreement the following afternoon, but that still left Lynette and her team working late the rest of the week, and probably Saturday, because Guy's delays delayed their work. Lynette was a stickler with staying as close to deadline as possible when it came to projects like this, but since this wasn't just updating someone's already built system but building one from scratch, she knew there were going to be issues and delays with either her buildout or even with the contractor, not due to a prima donna architect.

❖

Saturday afternoon Lynette trudged wearily back to her apartment after having her team come in at seven a.m. so that they could at least get as much done by noon as possible and still get to enjoy their first weekend in London. She, on the other hand, would be taking a much-needed nap for a few hours before she called Eve. As she approached the apartments, she could've sworn sleep deprivation had her seeing things because Eve couldn't possibly be sitting on a bench in front of the building with a suitcase beside her. Lynette closed her eyes, shook her head, opened them again, and almost cried out in relief when she saw Eve was still there. Eve took a step toward her, and Lynette practically ran to her and swept her up into a tight embrace.

"It is you! I'm not hallucinating?" she said as she was enveloped in Eve's seductive scent.

Eve's arms were wrapped just as tightly around her. "Yes, it's really me. I was tired of waiting for your call."

Lynette heard the emotion combined with humor in Eve's tone. She released her just enough to be able to look at her. "I'm sorry."

Eve gave her a soft smile. "You don't have to apologize. You're working, I told you I understood."

Lynette shook her head. "Not about that. About everything else. I'm so sorry for not being open with you about how I was feeling about Marisol, for you having to walk in on us like that, and for giving up on us so quickly."

Eve took Lynette's face in her warm, soft hands. "Again, you have nothing to apologize for. I'm the one that should be apologizing. I'm sorry for not giving you the chance to explain, for pushing you away instead of trying to understand, and for making you feel as if you had done something wrong. I've never loved anyone this way before, so this is all new to me."

Lynette's heart swelled at Eve's admission. She reached up, grasped one of Eve's hands, and placed a kiss on her palm. "Let's go to my room and talk."

Eve nodded and turned to grab the handle of her roll-away. Lynette opened the door, took the suitcase, and led Eve through the lobby to the elevator. She still couldn't believe Eve was there and was too afraid of letting her hand go to press the elevator button, so she just released the suitcase handle and used that hand. Lynette held on to Eve until they reached her apartment when she realized she was going to have to let Eve's hand go to open the door.

Eve must have noticed her hesitancy because she smiled and said, "I'm not going anywhere."

Lynette smiled in embarrassment and finally released Eve's hand. They were barely through the door before Lynette pulled Eve back into her arms. "I just need to hold you for a little while longer."

Eve rubbed her hand up and down Lynette's back. "I don't mind."

They stood that way for a moment, then Lynette did what she had ached to do the moment she'd pulled Eve into her arms downstairs. She grasped Eve's face and gently laid her lips upon Eve's. Eve whimpered and deepened the kiss within seconds of their lips touching. The kiss was filled with a need that went far beyond physical satisfaction. Lynette tried to put everything she hadn't been able to say in the past week into it, and Eve returned it just as passionately before she pulled away.

"We need to talk," Eve said breathlessly.

Lynette knew she was right, but all she wanted to do was strip Eve naked right there and make up for all the time lost between them. "Okay." She led Eve over to the sofa.

"How did you know where to find me?" Lynette asked as soon as they were seated.

"Your sister," Eve said guiltily.

Lynette chuckled. "Why am I not surprised."

"I just needed to see you in person. I didn't want to talk about something so important over the phone. Especially when I wouldn't be able to see you for weeks after."

Lynette gave Eve's hand a gentle squeeze. "I understand and agree. I just wish you hadn't had to fly across an ocean to do it."

"Well, I've always wanted to go to London. What better excuse to do it than to win back the woman I love?" Eve brushed her fingers across Lynette's cheek.

"I love you too, Eve. Whatever confusion and doubts I had about Marisol are gone. You're who I want to be with, who I want to build a life and future with. I don't ever want you to doubt the truth of that. If you ever do, tell me so I can reassure you that there's only you."

Unshed tears sparkled in Eve's eyes as she smiled happily. "It means the world to me to hear you say that. I've never loved anyone more than I love you. Even when I was married to Stefan, I could never see our future together. I just moved along year after year, feeling as if I was waiting for something, or someone, to come along to make me feel a passion and love I had only seen between my parents. I had no idea it was possible to feel this strongly for anyone until you came into my life and had me believing that what I'd been waiting for all along was you."

Lynette gently wiped away Eve's tears, feeling her own eyes tearing up with a happiness she couldn't contain. "Are we finished talking?" she asked, only half joking.

Eve chuckled. "I think so."

"Good."

Lynette stood, pulling Eve up with her, then bent over and picked Eve up into her arms. Eve squealed and locked her hands around Lynette's neck. Once Eve was securely in her arms, Lynette carried her into the bedroom, laid her on the bed, and quickly joined her.

"I've missed you so much," she said, spreading out Eve's curly locks on the pillow.

Eve softly stroked Lynette's cheek. "I've missed you too."

Lynette lowered her head for a kiss so slow and tender it made her heart ache. She didn't want to rush this moment. Wanted to savor every bit of it to remind her of what she almost lost. She and Eve were both entering new territory. She was learning how to surrender to love again. Eve was learning what being in love was genuinely like. Lynette knew there would probably be more bumps for them along the way, but she hoped they wouldn't be as big as this one. She couldn't bear the thought of almost losing Eve again.

She slowly undressed Eve, stroking and kissing every bit of flesh revealed with each item of clothing removed. As Eve lay writhing and moaning beneath her, her arousal permeated the air and Lynette breathed it in as if it was her life's breath. She hurriedly undressed as well and stretched her body partially atop Eve's, reaching down and sliding her hand between Eve's thighs.

"You feel so good," Lynette whispered against Eve's lips as she dipped a finger into Eve's warmth.

Eve moaned loudly in response as Lynette stroked her until the liquid warmth of her excitement coated her finger. She slid a second finger inside Eve to join the first and lowered her head to take a pebble hard nipple into her mouth. Eve sucked in a breath and her hips rose off the bed. Lynette stroked Eve until it felt as if she were delving into liquid fire. Eve's hips moved more frantically, and Lynette could feel her inner walls contract around her fingers. She slowed her hand to a stop but didn't withdraw.

"Please," Eve said breathlessly.

Lynette left Eve's breast and whispered in her ear, "Not yet."

Eve's only argument was a whimper. Lynette wouldn't let her suffer for long. Her own arousal was almost too much to bear. She eased her fingers from between Eve's womanly lips and made her way down Eve's body with her lips and tongue. By the time she settled between Eve's legs, she was writhing and moaning once again. Lynette inhaled the scent of Eve's arousal, almost causing her to reach her own orgasm. She lowered her head and dipped her tongue in Eve's cleft and slowly, methodically, made love to Eve until she was grasping Lynette's head and pumping her hips into her face as her orgasm flooded Lynette's mouth and soaked the bed covering beneath her.

Eve's body hadn't even stopped quaking from the aftershock of her orgasm when Lynette felt her tugging at her shoulders. She gazed up past Eve's torso to meet her passion-glazed eyes.

"Come here," Eve said hoarsely.

Lynette moved up to lay beside her, but Eve shook her head. "Straddle me," Eve said as she added another pillow beneath her head.

Lynette did as Eve asked. She'd barely settled above her before Eve grasped Lynette's hips and encouraged her lower until her lips were wrapped around Lynette's clit and coaxing moans from her now. Lynette grasped the headboard and did her best not to grind herself against Eve's face as her tongue did things that had her calling out Eve's name and almost ripping the headboard off. When Eve slid a finger into Lynette as she focused back on sucking her clit, Lynette felt as if her body was shattering into a million pieces as an intense orgasm rocked through her.

Afterward, with both panting, sweating, and covered in each other's scent, Lynette lay beside Eve, pulled her into her arms, and fell into a contented sleep.

❖

Eve watched Lynette sleep, still not believing she was here beside her. After Lynette's text a few days ago asking if they could delay their conversation, she had originally been fine with it. After all, Eve had made the same suggestion when she and Lynette had first spoken and been interrupted, but then panic set in that waiting too long would do more harm than good. The idea to hop on a plane to London had been one of those "if I were crazy" thoughts until she realized she probably could go to London. Make one of those grand romantic gesture movie moments where one of the main characters flew to the other side of the world to win back the other main character's heart. She double-checked her calendar and realized she had a whole week free of meetings and events. But the idea began losing momentum when she realized a last-minute flight was not going to be cheap. Then, as if the universe knew what was in her heart, one of her clients forwarded their signed contract and their deposit payment for their event sooner than she had expected.

Despite the sudden good fortune, Eve still felt the need to at least talk to someone who would tell her she was being too crazy and talk some sense into her. She called Paige, and to Eve's surprise, the woman who believed romance movies were a crock of shit loved the idea. She even had her assistant find flights for her after Eve spoke to Michelle, who happily gave her the address where Lynette was staying. From that point on, it all happened so fast Eve only had enough time to pack essentials into a suitcase and say good-bye to Juliana, who promised to explain to the rest of the family why she would be missing Sunday dinner. Eve felt bad leaving Juliana to face the entire Monroe clan alone, but she assured Eve she would be fine. She'd known most of the Monroe boys since they were in diapers, she could handle anything they threw at her.

Eve had been a nervous wreck the entire trip over worrying about the possibility that Lynette might not even want to see her. She was expecting a phone conversation, not a surprise, in-person confrontation. Her flight had arrived early in the morning and Eve felt bad enough just showing up unannounced, but to come knocking on Lynette's door at the crack of dawn was out of the question, so she found an airport kiosk just opening and sat in the terminal nursing a cup of coffee for two hours as she tried to figure out what she was going to say to Lynette.

Finally, too antsy to sit any longer, she grabbed a taxi and forty-five minutes later was standing in front of the address where Lynette was staying. She had buzzed the apartment number Michelle had given her on the intercom and waited for a response, but there was nothing. She tried a couple more times and considered calling or texting Lynette, then thought better of it. Maybe she had a late night and was still asleep, or she went into work, which wouldn't be surprising as Lynette sometimes worked weekends at home. Eve had walked around the neighborhood, found a little café, and managed to avoid the inevitable for another hour. She'd returned to the apartment just as Lynette had shown up. Eve had never been so anxious to see someone in her life. Then Lynette had rushed over and enveloped her in her strong embrace, and it had felt to Eve as if all were right with her world again.

She lifted a hand to smooth across Lynette's cheek, then changed her mind. Despite the smiles and passionate lovemaking, Eve hadn't missed noticing how tired Lynette had looked, so she didn't wake her. She eased out of bed, made a necessary trip to the bathroom, borrowed a robe that hung on the bathroom door, and went out onto the balcony of the apartment. It was early evening, and the streets below were bustling with activity. Although Eve looked forward to exploring London, with its surprising mixture of charming brick streets and buildings beside glass and steel encased high-rises, she would gladly settle for spending her week shut in the apartment whiling the hours away in bed with Lynette. As if she'd heard Eve's thoughts, Lynette's arms wrapped around her waist.

"When I woke up and found you gone, I thought I had dreamed the whole thing," Lynette said, her lips grazing Eve's earlobe sending tingles of pleasure throughout her body.

Eve turned her head to capture Lynette's lips with her own. "Does that feel like a dream?" she asked.

Lynette's lips split into a wide grin. "I think I may need more proof."

She turned Eve around and slipped her hands beneath the robe. Her eyes widened in surprise as her hands met bare flesh.

Eve quirked a brow. "Well?"

"Oh, definitely real." Her hands ran along Eve's waist to her lower back and down to her behind, grasping a handful.

"Unless you plan on giving your neighbors a show, I think we should take this inside." Eve cocked her head in the direction of a woman trying to make it look like she was reading her book instead of peeking at them over the top of it.

Lynette grinned mischievously. "Hey, Carol."

Her hands were still inside Eve's robe resting on her behind. Eve bit her bottom lip to keep from laughing.

The woman gazed up, a blush spreading throughout her face. "Oh…uh…hey, boss."

"Enjoy that book," Lynette said, wrapping her arm around Eve's waist and walking them back into the apartment.

They both laughed as Lynette closed the screen but left the glass door open.

"You are so bad," Eve said.

"Hey, I'm not the one walking around practically naked." Lynette gave her a look of pure innocence as she untied the robe and slid it off her shoulders and down her arms until it lay in a puddle at her feet.

Eve grasped the waistband of the shorts Lynette had put on and slid her hand into them. Her fingers met Lynette's smooth mound. "It looks like someone else left some clothing behind."

She dipped her fingers farther down to find Lynette slick with arousal. Lynette's eyes shuttered closed and she moaned deeply as Eve stroked until her fingers were just as slick as Lynette's sex. Eve eased her hand from between Lynette's thighs, and Lynette grasped her face for a kiss that left her dizzy. It took her a moment to realize Lynette was backing her toward the sofa. She brought an arm down to brace Eve as she lowered her to the cushions. The care with which Lynette treated her aroused Eve even more. She felt delicate and treasured when Lynette was so gentle with her. When Lynette ended the kiss, she straightened and looked down at Eve with an awed expression.

"I still can't believe you're here."

"I'm here." Eve offered Lynette a hand. "I guess I'll have to keep proving it to you until you believe it."

Lynette quickly shed her shorts and tank top and joined Eve on the sofa where she did her best to prove that this wasn't a dream.

❖

"I can't believe a week has come and gone so quickly," Lynette said, frowning.

"Me too. I wish I didn't have to go back so soon, but I have a meeting with the contractor working on my office and a client referral from Paige in two days."

"I wish I could've spent more time with you. I hate that you flew all this way to be with me and end up being alone for most of the time."

Eve gave her an understanding smile. "It's okay. I showed up unannounced. I didn't expect you to shirk your work to be with me. Besides, it was fun exploring the city on my own. Maybe next time we can come together on vacation or something."

Smiling, Lynette reached across the table to take Eve's hand. "I like hearing you say *we* in reference to future vacation plans."

"And I like saying it."

"So, what would you like to do on your last full day in London?"

Lynette's heart ached a little asking Eve that. A week ago, she was tired, miserable, and wondering if she would ever be happy again. Then she found Eve waiting on her doorstep and it was as if everything in her world seemed brighter and more beautiful. Even dealing with Guy wasn't so bad anymore. Her team noticed the difference in her demeanor as soon as she'd walked into the office the Monday after Eve had arrived with a bright smile cheerfully greeting them and asking about their weekend. Her project coordinator Carol, who had met Eve the following day after seeing them on the patio, knew why the smile was there but kept it to herself. Lynette never realized how one person could affect your life so deeply. It was as if she hadn't really been living life until Eve came into hers. It scared her and made her unbelievably happy at the same time.

"I'd like to go back to Covent Garden and then the London Eye."

"Excellent choices." Lynette signaled their server for the check, and a few minutes later they were on the Underground heading to their destination.

Lynette wanted to make sure Eve's last day would be memorable. She'd already known that Eve wanted to revisit Covent Garden and the Eye from a conversation they had after Eve's first visits to the attractions earlier in the week, so Lynette made a few arrangements to make this time more special. First, they visited Atelier Cologne where Lynette arranged for Eve to have a personal consultation to define her own personal scent. Then it was off to Burberry for a mini shopping spree to add to Eve's burgeoning bag collection. From there it was Happy Socks for Lynette's own pleasure, then a visit to the British Museum, a traditional British lunch at Battersea Pie Station, a shared dessert of an outrageously large cone of gelato from Venchi, and a matinee at the London Theatre before heading to the South Bank where the London Eye was located.

"Maybe we should've come here first," Eve said, frowning at the long line of people waiting to ride the massive Ferris wheel.

"No, the best time to go is at nightfall when you can see the lights of the city. Fortunately, I anticipated you wanting to come back, so I have something special planned."

Lynette looped Eve's arm through hers and led her away from the line to a separate entryway where she presented their tickets and was directed to the Eye Lounge.

Eve gazed curiously around. "I've had so many surprises today from you I'm not sure how many more I can handle."

Lynette grinned. "This is the last one, I promise. Why don't we get a cocktail? They'll come and get us when everything is ready."

They settled at the bar, ordered drinks, and talked about their day before a host came to escort them to their private capsule where they were greeted with appetizers and champagne service.

Eve looked at Lynette in surprise. "You arranged for all of this?"

"Yes. Since this was your first trip to London and we won't be seeing each other for another two to three weeks if we stay on track with this project, I wanted to make our last night together special." Lynette handed her a glass of champagne.

Eve's eyes sparkled with tears. "This whole day...whole week...has been like a dream."

Lynette held Eve's hand as she held up her glass of champagne. "Let's toast to making more dreams come true... together."

"Together," Eve said, touching her glass to Lynette's.

They both took a sip and walked over to look out the glass wall of the capsule as it ascended the wheel. Lynette wrapped her arm around Eve's waist.

Eve wrapped hers around Lynette's and laid her head on Lynette's shoulder. "This is breathtaking."

Lynette gazed down at Eve. "Yes, it is."

They munched on their appetizers and let the champagne flow as they rode the Ferris wheel. When they reached the top and their carriage stopped for them to admire the 360-degree view of the city of London, Lynette thought about her original plans for this trip before the Marisol situation happened. Ironically, the nightfall ride on the London Eye had been a part of her original plans, but this moment, as they sat atop the wheel, Lynette had planned to propose to Eve. Now that she looked back on the past several weeks and the hit their almost too perfect relationship took, she realized she would've been rushing into things too soon. They had only been together for a little over six months and still had so much more to discover not only about each other but themselves. She hated to admit it, but maybe what happened had been for the best to keep them from rushing in too soon and not learning to appreciate just being together.

"What are you thinking about?" Eve asked.

Lynette placed a soft kiss on Eve's lips. "How much I love us. How much I love you."

Eve reached up and stroked Lynette's cheek. "I love you too. I know the past few weeks haven't been easy, but I wouldn't change a thing as long as it led me back to you this way."

Lynette smiled down at the woman that had become her heart, her world. "I wouldn't either."

The scenic view was forgotten as their lips met, and Lynette wondered what the future held for them.

Chapter Twelve

Lynette couldn't believe the turnout. She had no idea this first of her Jessica Hart detective series novels would blow up the way it had. This was her first major signing since the release over a month ago, and all she could think about was Eve. She'd been the one encouraging Lynette to finish them, reading her drafts, lovingly pushing her to get past the blocks. Eve had been her inspiration, and Lynette wanted so much for her to be here standing beside her, but she knew that wasn't possible.

Lost in thought, Lynette barely gazed up as she was handed another book to sign. "Who should I sign this to?"

"To Eve."

Lynette stopped mid-stroke as she looked up into Eve's beautiful bright eyes. The moment felt almost surreal to Lynette, as if she'd experienced it before.

She smiled broadly. "Is there anything in particular you'd like me to write?"

"Yes. To Eve, the love of my life."

Lynette signed it just as Eve requested, then handed it back to her. "I thought you weren't going to be able to make it."

"I didn't think so either, but my client meeting finished early."

"That was the last one, Ms. Folsom," Lynette's assistant told her.

"Thank goodness. I don't think I could've signed another book." Lynette flexed her fingers as she came around the table.

Eve took her hand, massaging it gently. "Do you want to go out to dinner to celebrate your big success?"

Lynette's body reacted to the innocent touch in a not-so-innocent way. "I'd rather have a more private celebration."

Eve grinned. "Is that all you think about?"

"Only when I'm with you." Lynette brushed her lips across Eve's. "Let me finish up here then we can head home."

As she finished up with her assistant and the bookstore manager, Lynette found herself wondering where they would be now if Eve had given up on them instead of flying across the globe to fight for her. It was the most romantic thing anyone had ever done for her and reminded her of those movies she'd always made fun of but secretly loved. Now, a year later, their relationship had grown and was stronger than ever. Lynette knew the key to it was continuing to be just as open and honest with each other as they were when they began dating, whether they wanted to hear it or not. They had even taken a big step a few months ago by moving in together. Since Lynette had the bigger apartment, Eve had moved in with her and was renting her condo to Juliana. With the success of her new book, the promotion at her job, Eve's business booming since she opened her office, and how well they were doing living together, Lynette felt as if her life had become a dream that she never wanted to awaken from. She hoped, after tonight, Eve felt the same way.

❖

When they arrived home, Eve was surprised to enter a candlelit apartment with the aromatic scent of food being prepared filling the air and their small dining table set up for a romantic dinner for two.

She looked back at Lynette with a broad smile. "I'm assuming this is what you meant by a private celebration."

Lynette grinned mischievously. "Surprised?"

"Very."

"Good."

Eve wrapped her arms around Lynette's waist. "You're amazing, you know that?"

"I know," Lynette said with a wink. "Now, sit down and have a glass of wine. I'll be right back."

Eve admired Lynette's firm, jean-clad behind as she walked away, reminding her of the night they had met at her book release party. Everything shifted that night because she'd met the woman who would change her whole life. Meeting Lynette not only meant finding and accepting who she was, but also finding a true and honest love. With a contented sigh, Eve walked over to the dining table. A bottle of wine chilled in an ice bucket beside it. She poured two glasses as Lynette and a chef she recognized from one of Details by Eve's catering partners brought out their meal.

"I can't believe you arranged all of this without me knowing," Eve said.

"I realized I've been so busy with the promotion and the book being released that I've been neglecting you, so I thought you deserved some spoiling tonight. This is just the beginning." Lynette grinned.

After dinner, Lynette surprised Eve further by drawing her a bubble bath complete with champagne and strawberries and insisted she relax while Lynette cleaned up. Eve came out of the bathroom to a trail of flower petals leading to the bedroom where candles from the living room had been moved to, John Legend crooning "All of Me," and Lynette kneeling at the foot of the bed holding a ring box where a gorgeous diamond and sapphire engagement ring lay amongst a bed of black satin. Eve looked in open-mouthed shock from the ring to Lynette, who looked so sexy and confident in what she was about to do.

"Eve, from the moment I saw you something told me I couldn't let you get away, and there hasn't been a day since that I regret listening to that voice. You've shown me how to love again, that I'm worthy of being loved, and have made me a better person. I know we started out with some bumps in the road, but as easy as it is to travel a smooth road, the bumps and potholes give it character. I want to spend the rest of my life not only creating the bumps but working together to smooth them out, to love you in every way you deserve to be loved, and to be loved by you. Will you marry me?"

Eve knelt in front of Lynette, head nodding, tears blurring her vision, and her heart feeling as if it were about to burst from joy. "Yes," she whispered, her voice too caught up in emotion to speak any louder. If she could, she would've shouted it from the rooftop of the building.

Lynette's eyes also teared up as she took the ring from the box and placed it on Eve's finger.

"A perfect fit. Just like us," Lynette said, her voice also choked with emotion.

Eve gazed down at the ring on her finger then back up at Lynette and took her face in her hands.

"I love you, Lynette Folsom, and I can't wait to profess that love and my commitment to you before anybody and everybody that will listen." Eve leaned forward and kissed a salty tear from Lynette's cheek then her lips.

They quickly undressed and were a passionate tangle

of lips and limbs as they climbed into bed, but after a few minutes, Lynette slowed the momentum. Eve cried at the tenderness of Lynette's lovemaking. It was as if it were their first time again. Every nerve ending in Eve's body came alive as Lynette would bring her to the peak of pleasure several times before finally giving her a release so intense that she'd thought she'd died and gone to heaven. Afterward, they lay tired but content within each other's arms, and Eve wondered how she could've been so lucky to have found something so wonderfully beautiful.

Lynette placed a soft kiss on her forehead. "Have I told you how much I love you?"

"Yes, but I don't mind hearing it again."

"Oh, in that case," Lynette propped her head on her hand and gazed into Eve's eyes, "Eve Monroe, I couldn't imagine loving anyone as much as I love you. There's nothing your heart desires that I wouldn't search the world to find."

With a tearful smile, Eve lovingly stroked Lynette's cheek. "I love you too, and there's no need to search the world because everything I could ever possibly desire is right here in my arms."

About the Author

Anne Shade loves writing stories about women who love women featuring strong, beautiful BIPOC characters. Anne is the author of four novels under Bold Strokes Books: *Femme Tales*, queered retellings of three classic fairytales and short-listed for a 2021 Lambda Literary Award; *Masquerade*, a Roaring Twenties romance; *Love and Lotus Blossoms*, a coming of age and coming out story and featured on Publishers Weekly Best Books of 2021 list. Anne has also collaborated with editor Victoria Villaseñor for the Bold Strokes Books anthology *In Our Words: Queer Stories from Black, Indigenous and People of Color*. When Anne isn't busy writing she's crafting and making plans for her future bed & breakfast.

Books Available From Bold Strokes Books

Deadly Secrets by VK Powell. Corporate criminals want whistleblower Jana Elliott permanently silenced, but Rafe Silva will risk everything to keep the woman she loves safe. (978-1-63679-087-9)

Enchanted Autumn by Ursula Klein. When Elizabeth comes to Salem, Massachusetts, to study the witch trials, she never expects to find love—or an actual witch…and Hazel might just turn out to be both. (978-1-63679-104-3)

Escorted by Renee Roman. When fantasy meets reality, will escort Ryan Lewis be able to walk away from a chance at forever with her new client Dani? (978-1-63679-039-8)

Her Heart's Desire by Anne Shade. Two women. One choice. Will Eve and Lynette be able to overcome their doubts and fears to embrace their deepest desire? (978-1-63679-102-9)

My Secret Valentine by Julie Cannon, Erin Dutton & Anne Shade. Winning the heart of your secret Valentine? These award-winning authors agree, there is no better way to fall in love. (978-1-63679-071-8)

Perilous Obsession by Carsen Taite. When reporter Macy Moran becomes consumed with solving a cold case, will her quest for the truth bring her closer to Detective Beck Ramsey or will her obsession with finding a murderer rob her of a chance at true love? (978-1-63679-009-1)

Reading Her by Amanda Radley. Lauren and Allegra learn love and happiness are right where they least expect it. There's just one problem: Lauren has a secret she cannot tell anyone, and Allegra knows she's hiding something. (978-1-63679-075-6)

The Willing by Lyn Hemphill. Kitty Wilson doesn't know how, but she can bring people back from the dead as long as someone is willing to take their place and keep the universe in balance. (978-1-63679-083-1)

Watching Over Her by Ronica Black. As they face the snowstorm of the century, and the looming threat of a stalker, Riley and Zoey just might find love in the most unexpected of places. (978-1-63679-100-5)

Always by Kris Bryant. When a pushy American private investigator shows up demanding to meet the woman in Camila's artwork, instead of introducing her to her great-grandmother, Camila decides to lead her on a wild goose chase all over Italy. (978-1-63679-027-5)

Exes and O's by Joy Argento. Ali and Madison really only have one thing in common. The girl who broke their heart may be the only one who can put it back together. (978-1-63679-017-6)

Paris Rules by Jaime Maddox. Carly Becker has been searching for the perfect woman all her life, but no one ever seems to be just right until Paige Waterford checks all her boxes, except the most important one—she's married. (978-1-63679-077-0)

Shadow Dancers by Suzie Clarke. In this third and final book in the Moon Shadow series, Rachel must find a way to become the hunter and not the hunted, and this time she will meet Eshee Yumiko head-on. (978-1-63555-829-6)

The Kiss by C.A. Popovich. When her wife refuses their divorce and begins to stalk her, threatening her life, Kate realizes to protect her new love, Leslie, she has to let her go, even if it breaks her heart. (978-1-63679-079-4)

The Wedding Setup by Charlotte Greene. When Ryann, a big-time New York executive, goes to Colorado to help out with her best friend's wedding, she never expects to fall for the maid of honor. (978-1-63679-033-6)

Velocity by Gun Brooke. Holly and Claire work toward an uncertain future preparing for an alien space mission, and only one thing is certain—they will have to risk their lives, and their hearts, to discover the truth. (978-1-63555-983-5)

Wildflower Words by Sam Ledel. Lida Jones treks west with her father in search of a better life on the rapidly developing American frontier, but finds home when she meets Hazel Thompson. (978-1-63679-055-8)